Edgar Allan Poe's
Tales of Science Fiction

-

A Collection of
Short Stories

British Library Cataloguing-in-Publication Data
A catalogue record for this book is available from the
British Library

Contents

Edgar Allan Poe

Edgar Allan Poe was born in Boston, Massachusetts in 1809. He was left an orphan at a very young age, following the abscondence of his father and subsequent death of his mother, but was taken in by a couple from Richmond, Virginia. After a brief spell living in England and Scotland, Poe enrolled at the newly-established University of Virginia. However, after just one semester, having become estranged from his foster father due to gambling debts, and finding himself unable to fund his studies, he dropped out. In 1827, aged 18, Poe travelled back to Boston, the city of his birth.

By now in severe financial trouble, Poe lied about his age in order to enlist in the army. After spending two years posted to South Carolina, and having failed as an officer's cadet at West Point, Poe left the military by getting deliberately court-martialled. He left for New York in 1831, where he released his third collection of poems, the first two having received almost zero attention. Not long after its publication, in March of 1831, Poe returned to Baltimore.

From 1831 onwards, Poe began in earnest to try and make a living as a writer, and turned from poetry to prose. Despite often finding himself penniless, and frequently having to move city to stay in employment as a critic, during the thirties and forties Poe published a good amount of fiction. Most of his best known short-stories, such as 'The Tell Tale Heart,' 'Ligeia', 'William Wilson' and 'The Fall of the House of Usher', were published between 1835 and 1845. In January 1845, Poe published his poem 'The Raven', which – despite fact that he only received $9 for it – was a great success, turning him overnight into something of a household name.

Poe died in 1849, aged just 40. The circumstances were somewhat odd; he was found wandering the streets of Baltimore at five in the morning, delirious and wearing someone else's clothes, and he repeatedly cried out "Reynolds!" during the hours before his death. The cause of death remains a mystery, with everything from epilepsy to rabies cited. However, whatever the reason behind his unusual passing, Poe's legacy is a formidable one: He is seen today as one of the greatest practitioners of Gothic and detective fiction that ever lived, and popular culture is replete with references to him.

The Unparalleled Adventure of One Hans Pfaall

With a heart of furious fancies,
Whereof I am commander,
With a burning spear and a horse of air,
To the wilderness I wander.
Tom O'Bedlam's Song.

BY late accounts from Rotterdam, that city seems to be in a high state of philosophical excitement. Indeed, phenomena have there occurred of a nature so completely unexpected — so entirely novel — so utterly at variance with preconceived opinions — as to leave no doubt on my mind that long ere this all Europe is in an uproar, all physics in a ferment, all reason and astronomy together by the ears.

It appears that on the —— day of ——, (I am not positive about the date,) a vast crowd of people, for purposes not specifically mentioned, were assembled in the great square of the Exchange in the well-conditioned city of Rotterdam. The day was warm — unusually so for the season — there was hardly a breath of air stirring; and the multitude were in no bad humor at being now and then besprinkled with friendly showers of momentary duration, that fell from large white masses of cloud profusely distributed about the blue vault of the firmament. Nevertheless, about noon, a slight but remarkable agitation became apparent in the assembly; the clattering of ten thousand tongues succeeded; and, in an instant afterwards, ten thousand faces were upturned towards the heavens, ten thousand pipes descended simultaneously from the corners of ten thousand mouths, and a shout, which could be compared to nothing but the roaring of Niagara, resounded long, loudly and furiously, through all the city and through all the environs of Rotterdam.

The origin of this hubbub soon became sufficiently evident. From behind the huge bulk of one of those sharply defined masses of cloud already mentioned, was seen slowly to emerge into an open area of blue space, a queer, heterogeneous, but apparently solid substance, so oddly shaped, so whimsically put together, as not to be in any manner comprehended, and never to be sufficiently admired, by the host of sturdy burghers who stood open-mouthed below. What could it be? In the name of all the devils in Rotterdam, what could it possibly portend? No one knew; no one could imagine; no one — not even the burgomaster Mynheer Superbus Von Underduk — had the slightest clew by which to unravel the mystery; so, as nothing more reasonable could be done, every one to a man replaced his pipe carefully in the corner of his mouth, and maintaining an eye steadily upon the phenomenon, puffed, paused, waddled about, and grunted significantly — then waddled back, grunted, paused, and finally — puffed again.

In the meantime, however, lower and still lower towards the goodly city, came the object of so much curiosity, and the cause of so much smoke. In a very few minutes it arrived near enough to be accurately discerned. It appeared to be — yes! it was undoubtedly a species of balloon; but surely no such balloon had ever been seen in Rotterdam before. For who, let me ask, ever heard of a balloon manufactured entirely of dirty newspapers? No man in Holland certainly; yet here, under the very noses of the people, or rather at some distance above their noses, was the identical thing in question, and composed, I have it on the best authority, of the precise material which no one had ever before known to be used for a similar purpose. — It was an egregious insult to the good sense of the burghers of Rotterdam. As to the shape of the phenomenon, it was even still more reprehensible. Being little or nothing better than a huge fool's-cap turned upside down. And this similitude was regarded as by no means lessened, when upon nearer inspection, the crowd saw a large tassel depending from its apex, and, around the upper rim or base of the cone, a circle of little instruments, resembling sheep-bells, which kept up a continual tinkling to the tune of Betty Martin. — But still worse. Suspended by blue ribbons to the end of this fantastic machine, there hung, by way of car, an enormous drab beaver hat, with a brim superlatively broad, and a hemispherical crown with a black band and a silver buckle. It is, however, somewhat remarkable that many citizens of Rotterdam swore to having seen the same hat repeatedly before; and indeed the whole assembly seemed to regard it with eyes of familiarity; while the vrow Grettel Pfaall, upon sight of it, uttered an exclamation of joyful surprise, and declared it to be the identical hat of her good man himself. Now this was a circumstance the more to be observed, as Pfaall, with three companions, had actually disappeared from Rotterdam about five years before, in a very sudden and unaccountable manner, and up to the date of this narrative all attempts at obtaining intelligence concerning them had failed. To be sure, some bones which were thought to be human, mixed up with a quantity of odd-looking rubbish, had been lately discovered in a retired situation to the east of the city; and some people went so far as to imagine that in this spot a foul murder had been committed, and that the sufferers were in all probability Hans Pfaall and his associates. — But to return.

The balloon (for such no doubt it was) had now descended to within a hundred feet of the earth, allowing the crowd below a sufficiently distinct view of the person of its occupant. This was in truth a very singular somebody. He could not have been more than two feet in height; but this altitude, little as it was, would have been sufficient to destroy his equilibrium, and tilt him over the edge of his tiny car, but for the intervention of a circular rim reaching as high as the breast, and rigged on to the cords of the balloon. The body of the little man was more than proportionally broad, giving to his entire figure a rotundity highly absurd. His feet, of course, could not be seen at all. His hands were enormously large. His hair was gray, and collected into a queue behind. His nose was prodigiously long, crooked and inflammatory; his eyes full, brilliant, and acute; his chin and cheeks, although wrinkled with age, were broad, puffy, and double; but of ears of any kind there was not a semblance to be discovered upon any portion of his head. This odd little gentleman was dressed in a loose surtout of sky-blue satin, with tight breeches to match, fastened with silver buckles at the knees. His vest was of some bright yellow material; a white taffety cap was set jauntily on one side of his head; and, to complete his equipment, a blood-red silk handkerchief enveloped his throat, and fell down, in a dainty manner, upon his bosom, in a fantastic bow-knot of super-eminent dimensions.

Having descended, as I said before, to about one hundred feet from the surface of the earth, the little old gentleman was suddenly seized with a fit of trepidation, and appeared disinclined to make any nearer approach to terra firma. Throwing out, therefore, a quantity of sand from a canvass bag, which he lifted with great difficulty, he became stationary in an instant. He then proceeded in a hurried and agitated manner, to extract from a side-pocket in his surtout a large morocco pocket-book. This he poised suspiciously in his hand; then eyed it with an air of extreme surprise, and was evidently astonished at its weight. He at length opened it, and, drawing therefrom a huge letter sealed with red sealing-wax and tied carefully with red tape, let it fall precisely at the feet of the burgomaster Superbus Von Underduk. His Excellency stooped to take it up. But the æronaut, still greatly discomposed, and having apparently no further business to detain him in Rotterdam, began at this moment to make busy preparations for departure; and, it being necessary to discharge a portion of ballast to enable him to reascend, the half dozen bags which he threw out, one after another, without taking the trouble to empty their contents, tumbled, every one of them, most unfortunately, upon the back of the burgomaster, and rolled him over and over no less than half a dozen times, in the face of every individual in Rotterdam. It is not to be supposed, however, that the great Underduk suffered this impertinence on the part of the little old man to pass off with impunity. It is said, on the contrary, that during each of his half dozen circumvolutions, he omitted no less than half a dozen distinct and furious whiffs from his pipe, to which he held fast the whole time with all his might, and to which he intends holding fast, (God willing,) until the day of his decease.

In the meantime the balloon arose like a lark, and, soaring far away above the city, at length drifted quietly behind a cloud similar to that from which it had so oddly emerged, and was thus lost forever to the wondering eyes of the good citizens of Rotterdam. All attention was now directed to the letter, the descent of which, and the consequences attending thereupon, had proved so fatally subversive of both person and personal dignity to his Excellency, Von Underduk. That functionary, however, had not failed, during his circumgyratory movements, to bestow a thought upon the important object of securing the epistle, which was seen, upon inspection, to have fallen into the most proper hands, being actually addressed to himself and Professor Rubadub, in their official capacities of President and Vice-President of the Rotterdam College of Astronomy. It was accordingly opened by those dignitaries upon the spot, and found to contain the following extraordinary, and indeed very serious, communication: — To their Excellencies Von Underduk and Rubadub, President and Vice-President of the States' College of Astronomers, in the city of Rotterdam.

Your Excellencies may perhaps be able to remember an humble artizan, by name Hans Pfaall, and by occupation a mender of bellows, who, with three others, disappeared from Rotterdam, about five years ago, in a manner which must have been considered unaccountable. If, however, it so please your Excellencies, I, the writer of this communication, am the identical Hans Pfaall himself. It is well known to most of my fellow-citizens, that for the period of forty years I continued to occupy the little square brick building, at the head of the alley called Sauerkraut, in which I resided at the time of my disappearance. My ancestors have also resided therein time out of mind — they, as well as myself, steadily following the respectable and indeed lucrative profession of mending of bellows: for, to speak the truth, until of late years, that the heads of all the people have been set agog with politics, no better business than my own could an honest citizen of Rotterdam either desire or deserve. Credit was good, employment was never wanting, and there was no lack of either money or good will. But, as I was saying, we soon began to feel the effects of liberty, and long speeches, and radicalism, and all that sort of thing. People who were formerly the very best customers in the world, had now not a moment of time to think of us at all. They had as much as they could do to read about the revolutions, and keep up with the march of intellect and the spirit of the age. If a fire wanted fanning, it could readily be fanned with a newspaper; and as the government grew weaker, I have no doubt that leather and iron acquired durability in proportion — for, in a very short time, there was not a pair of bellows in all Rotterdam that ever stood in need of a stitch or required the assistance of a hammer. This was a state of things not to be endured. I soon grew as poor as a rat, and, having a wife and children to provide for, my burdens at length became intolerable, and I spent hour after hour in reflecting upon the most convenient method of putting an end to my life. Duns, in the meantime, left me little leisure for contemplation. My house was literally besieged from morning till night. There were three fellows in particular, who worried me beyond endurance, keeping watch continually about my door, and threatening me with the law. Upon these three I vowed the bitterest revenge, if ever I should be so happy as to get them within my clutches; and I believe nothing in the world but the pleasure of this anticipation prevented me from putting my plan of suicide into immediate execution, by blowing my brains out with a blunderbuss. I thought it best, however, to dissemble my wrath, and to treat them with promises and fair words, until, by some good turn of fate, an opportunity of vengeance should be afforded me.

One day, having given them the slip, and feeling more than usually dejected, I continued for a long time to wander about the most obscure streets without object, until at length I chanced to stumble against the corner of a bookseller's stall. Seeing a chair close at hand, for the use of customers, I threw myself doggedly into it, and, hardly knowing why, opened the pages of the first volume which came within my reach. It proved to be a small pamphlet treatise on Speculative Astronomy, written either by Professor Encke of Berlin, or by a Frenchman of somewhat similar name. I had some little tincture of information on matters of this nature, and soon became more and more absorbed in the contents of the book — reading it actually through twice before I awoke to a recollection of what was passing around me. By this time it began to grow dark, and I directed my steps toward home. But the treatise (in conjunction with a discovery in pneumatics, lately communicated to me as an important secret, by a cousin from Nantz,) had made an indelible impression on my mind, and, as I sauntered along the dusky streets, I revolved carefully over in my memory the wild and sometimes unintelligible reasonings of the writer. There were some particular passages which affected my imagination in an extraordinary manner. The longer I meditated upon these, the more intense grew the interest which had been excited within me. The limited nature of my education in general, and more especially my ignorance on subjects connected with natural philosophy, so far from rendering me diffident of my own ability to comprehend what I had read, or inducing me to mistrust the many vague notions which had arisen in consequence, merely served as a farther stimulus to imagination; and I was vain enough, or perhaps reasonable enough, to doubt whether those crude ideas which, arising in ill-regulated minds, have all the appearance, may not often in effect possess all the force, the reality, and other inherent properties of instinct or intuition.

It was late when I reached home, and I went immediately to bed. My mind, however, was too much occupied to sleep, and I lay the whole night buried in meditation. Arising early in the morning, I repaired eagerly to the bookseller's stall, and laid out what little ready money I possessed, in the purchase of some volumes of Mechanics and Practical Astronomy. Having arrived at home safely with these, I devoted every spare moment to their perusal, and soon made such proficiency in studies of this nature as I thought sufficient for the execution of a certain design with which either the devil or my better genius had inspired me. In the intervals of this period, I made every endeavor to conciliate the three creditors who had given me so much annoyance. In this I finally succeeded — partly by selling enough of my household furniture to satisfy a moiety of their claim, and partly by a promise of paying the balance upon completion of a little project which I told them I had in view, and for assistance in which I solicited their services. By these means (for they were ignorant men) I found little difficulty in gaining them over to my purpose.

Matters being thus arranged, I contrived, by the aid of my wife, and with the greatest secrecy and caution, to dispose of what property I had remaining, and to borrow, in small sums, under various pretences, and without giving any attention (I am ashamed to say) to my future means of repayment, no inconsiderable quantity of ready money. With the means thus accruing I proceeded to procure at intervals, cambric muslin, very fine, in pieces of twelve yards each; twine; a lot of the varnish of caoutchouc; a large and deep basket of wicker-work, made to order; and several other articles necessary in the construction and equipment of a balloon of extraordinary dimensions. This I directed my wife to make up as soon as possible, and gave her all requisite information as to the particular method of proceeding. In the meantime I worked up the twine into net-work of sufficient dimensions; rigged it with a hoop and the necessary cords; and made purchase of numerous instruments and materials for experiment in the upper regions of the upper atmosphere. I then took opportunities of conveying by night, to a retired situation east of Rotterdam, five iron-bound casks, to contain about fifty gallons each, and one of a larger size; six tin tubes, three inches in diameter, properly shaped, and ten feet in length; a quantity of a particular metallic substance, or semi-metal which I shall not name, and a dozen demijohns of a very common acid. The gas to be formed from these latter materials is a gas never yet generated by any other person than myself — or at least never applied to any similar purpose. I can only venture to say here, that it is a constituent of azote, so long considered irreducible, and that its density is about 37.4 times less than that of hydrogen. It is tasteless, but not odorless; burns, when pure, with a greenish flame, and is instantaneously fatal to animal life. Its full secret I would make no difficulty in disclosing, but that it of right belongs (as I have before hinted) to a citizen of Nantz, in France, by whom it was conditionally communicated to myself. The same individual submitted to me, without being at all aware of my intentions, a method of constructing balloons from the membrane of a certain animal, through which substance any escape of gas was nearly an impossibility. I found it, however, altogether too expensive, and was not sure, upon the whole, whether cambric muslin with a coating of gum caoutchouc, was not equally as good. I mention this circumstance, because I think it probable that hereafter the individual in question may attempt a balloon ascension with the novel gas and material I have spoken of, and I do not wish to deprive him of the honor of a very singular invention.

On the spot which I intended each of the smaller casks to occupy respectively during the inflation of the balloon, I privately dug a small hole; the holes forming in this manner a circle twenty-five feet in diameter. In the centre of this circle, being the station designed for the large cask, I also dug a hole of greater depth. In each of the five smaller holes, I deposited a canister containing fifty pounds, and in the larger one a keg holding one hundred and fifty pounds of cannon powder. These — the keg and the canisters — I connected in a proper manner with covered trains; and having let into one of the canisters the end of about four feet of slow-match, I covered up the hole, and placed the cask over it, leaving the other end of the match protruding about an inch, and barely visible beyond the cask. I then filled up the remaining holes, and placed the barrels over them in their destined situation!

Besides the articles above enumerated, I conveyed to the

dépôt, and there secreted, one of M. Grimm's improvements upon the apparatus for condensation of the atmospheric air. I found this machine, however, to require considerable alteration before it could be adapted to the purposes to which I intended making it applicable. But, with severe labor and unremitting perseverance, I at length met with entire success in all my preparations. My balloon was soon completed. It would contain more than forty thousand cubic feet of gas; would take me up easily, I calculated, with all my implements, and, if I managed rightly, with one hundred and seventy-five pounds of ballast into the bargain. It had received three coats of varnish, and I found the cambric muslin to answer all the purposes of silk itself, being quite as strong and a good deal less expensive.

Everything being now ready, I exacted from my wife an oath of secrecy in relation to all my actions from the day of my first visit to the bookseller's stall; and promising, on my part, to return as soon as circumstances would permit, I gave her what little money I had left, and bade her farewell. Indeed I had no fear on her account. She was what people call a notable woman, and could manage matters in the world without my assistance. I believe, to tell the truth, she always looked upon me as an idle body — a mere make-weight — good for nothing but building castles in the air — and was rather glad to get rid of me. It was a dark night when I bade her good bye, and taking with me, as aides-de-camp, the three creditors who had given me so much trouble, we carried the balloon, with the car and accoutrements, by a roundabout way, to the station where the other articles were deposited. We there found them all unmolested, and I proceeded immediately to business.

It was the first of April. The night, as I said before, was dark; there was not a star to be seen; and a drizzling rain, falling at intervals, rendered us very uncomfortable. But my chief anxiety was concerning the balloon, which, in spite of the varnish with which it was defended, began to grow rather heavy with the moisture; the powder also was liable to damage. I therefore kept my three duns working with great diligence, pounding down ice around the central cask, and stirring the acid in the others. They did not cease, however, importuning me with questions as to what I intended to do with all this apparatus, and expressed much dissatisfaction at the terrible labor I made them undergo. They could not perceive (so they said) what good was likely to result from their getting wet to the skin, merely to take a part in such horrible incantations. I began to get uneasy, and worked away with all my might; for I verily believe the idiots supposed that I had entered into a compact with the devil, and that, in short, what I was now doing was nothing better than it should be. I was, therefore, in great fear of their leaving me altogether. I contrived, however, to pacify them by promises of payment of all scores in full, as soon as I could bring the present business to a termination. To these speeches they gave of course their own interpretation; fancying, no doubt, that at all events I should come into possession of vast quantities of ready money; and provided I paid them all I owed, and a trifle more, in consideration of their services, I dare say they cared very little what became of either my soul or my carcass.

In about four hours and a half I found the balloon sufficiently inflated. I attached the car, therefore, and put all my implements in it — a telescope; a barometer, with some important modifications; a thermometer; an electrometer; a compass; a magnetic needle; a seconds watch; a bell; a speaking trumpet, etc., etc., etc. — also a globe of glass, exhausted of air, and carefully closed with a stopper — not forgetting the condensing apparatus, some unslacked lime, a stick of sealing wax, a copious supply of water, and a large quantity of provisions, such as pemmican, in which much nutriment is contained in comparatively little bulk. I also secured in the car a pair of pigeons and a cat.

It was now nearly daybreak, and I thought it high time to take my departure. Dropping a lighted cigar on the ground, as if by accident, I took the opportunity, in stooping to pick it up, of igniting privately the piece of slow match, the end of which, as I said before, protruded a little beyond the lower rim of one of the smaller casks. This manœuvre was totally unperceived on the part of the three duns; and, jumping into the car, I immediately cut the single cord which held me to the earth, and was pleased to find that I shot upwards with inconceivable rapidity, carrying with all ease one hundred and seventy-five pounds of leaden ballast, and able to have carried up as many more. As I left the earth, the barometer stood at thirty inches, and the centigrade thermometer at 19°.

Scarcely, however, had I attained the height of fifty yards, when, roaring and rumbling up after me in the most tumultuous and terrible manner, came so dense a hurricane of fire, and gravel, and burning wood, and blazing metal, and mangled limbs, that my very heart sunk within me, and I fell down in the bottom of the car, trembling with terror. Indeed, I now perceived that I had entirely overdone the business, and that the main consequences of the shock were yet to be experienced. Accordingly, in less than a second, I felt all the blood in my body rushing to my temples, and, immediately thereupon, a concussion, which I shall never forget, burst abruptly through the night, and seemed to rip the very firmament asunder. When I afterwards had time for reflection, I did not fail to attribute the extreme violence of the explosion, as regarded myself, to its proper cause — my situation directly above it, and in the line of its greatest power. But at the time, I thought only of preserving my life. The balloon at first collapsed, then furiously expanded, then whirled round and round with sickening velocity, and finally, reeling and staggering like a drunken man, hurled me over the rim of the car, and left me dangling, at a terrific height, with my head downward, and my face outward, by a piece of slender cord about three feet in length, which hung accidentally through a crevice near the bottom of the wicker-work, and in which, as I fell, my left foot became most providentially entangled. It is impossible — utterly impossible — to form any adequate idea of the horror of my situation. I gasped convulsively for breath — a shudder resembling a fit of the ague agitated every nerve and muscle in my frame — I felt my eyes starting from their sockets — a horrible nausea overwhelmed me — and at length I lost all consciousness in a swoon.

How long I remained in this state it is impossible to say. It must, however, have been no inconsiderable time, for when I partially recovered the sense of existence, I found the day breaking, the balloon at a prodigious height over a wilderness of ocean, and not a trace of land to be discovered far and wide within the limits of the vast horizon. My sensations, however, upon thus recovering, were by no means so replete with agony as might have been anticipated. Indeed, there was much of madness in the calm survey which I began to take of my situation. I drew up to my eyes each of my hands, one after the other, and wondered what occurrence could have given rise to the swelling of the veins, and the horrible blackness of the finger nails. I afterwards carefully examined my head, shaking it repeatedly, and feeling it with minute attention, until I succeeded in satisfying myself that it was not, as I had more than half suspected, larger than my balloon. Then, in a knowing manner, I felt in both my breeches pockets, and, missing therefrom a set of tablets and a tooth-pick case, endeavored to account for their disappearance, and, not being able to do so, felt inexpressibly chagrined. It now occurred to me that I suffered great uneasiness in the joint of my left ankle, and a dim consciousness of my situation began to glimmer through my mind. But, strange to say! I was neither astonished nor horror-stricken. If I felt any emotion at all, it was a kind of chuckling satisfaction at the cleverness I was about to display in extricating myself from this dilemma; and never, for a moment, did I look upon my ultimate safety as a question susceptible of doubt. For a few minutes I remained wrapped in the profoundest meditation. I have a distinct recollection of frequently compressing my lips, putting my fore-finger to the side of my nose, and making use of other gesticulations and grimaces common to men who, at ease in their arm-chairs, meditate upon matters of intricacy or importance. Having, as I thought, sufficiently collected my ideas, I now, with great caution and deliberation, put my hands behind my back, and unfastened the large iron buckle which belonged to the waist-band of my pantaloons. This buckle had three teeth, which, being somewhat rusty, turned with great difficulty on their axis. I brought them, however, after some trouble, at right angles to the body of the buckle, and was glad to find them remain firm in that position. Holding within my teeth the instrument thus obtained, I now proceeded to untie the knot of my cravat. I had to rest several times before I could accomplish this manœuvre; but it was at length accomplished. To one end of the cravat I then made fast the buckle, and the other end I tied, for greater security, tightly around my wrist. Drawing now my body upwards, with a prodigious exertion of muscular force, I succeeded, at the very first trial, in throwing the buckle over the car, and entangling it, as I had anticipated, in the circular rim of the wicker-work.

My body was now inclined towards the side of the car,

at an angle of about forty-five degrees; but it must not be understood that I was therefore only forty-five degrees below the perpendicular. So far from it, I still lay nearly level with the plane of the horizon; for the change of situation which I had acquired, had forced the bottom of the car considerably outward from my position, which was accordingly one of the most imminent peril. It should be remembered, however, that when I fell, in the first instance, from the car, if I had fallen with my face turned toward the balloon, instead of turned outwardly from it as it actually was — or if, in the second place, the cord by which I was suspended had chanced to hang over the upper edge, instead of through a crevice near the bottom of the car — I say it may readily be conceived that, in either of these supposed cases, I should have been unable to accomplish even as much as I had now accomplished, and the disclosures now made would have been utterly lost to posterity. I had therefore every reason to be grateful; although, in point of fact, I was still too stupid to be any thing at all, and hung for, perhaps, a quarter of an hour, in that extraordinary manner, without making the slightest farther exertion, and in a singularly tranquil state of idiotic enjoyment. But this feeling did not fail to die rapidly away, and thereunto succeeded horror, and dismay, and a sense of utter helplessness and ruin. In fact, the blood so long accumulating in the vessels of my head and throat, and which had hitherto buoyed up my spirits with delirium, had now begun to retire within their proper channels, and the distinctness which was thus added to my perception of the danger, merely served to deprive me of the self-possession and courage to encounter it. But this weakness was, luckily for me, of no very long duration. In good time came to my rescue the spirit of despair, and, with frantic cries and struggles, I jerked my way bodily upwards, till, at length, clutching with a vice-like grip the long-desired rim, I writhed my person over it, and fell headlong and shuddering within the car.

It was not until some time afterward that I recovered myself sufficiently to attend to the ordinary cares of the balloon. I then, however, examined it with attention, and found it, to my great relief, uninjured. My implements were all safe, and, fortunately, I had lost neither ballast nor provisions. Indeed, I had so well secured them in their places, that such an accident was entirely out of the question. Looking at my watch, I found it six o'clock. I was still rapidly ascending, and the barometer gave a present altitude of three and three-quarter miles. Immediately beneath me in the ocean, lay a small black object, slightly oblong in shape, seemingly about the size of a domino, and in every respect bearing a great resemblance to one of those toys. Bringing my telescope to bear upon it, I plainly discerned it to be a British ninety-four gun ship, close-hauled, and pitching heavily in the sea with her head to the W. S. W. Besides this ship, I saw nothing but the ocean and the sky, and the sun, which had long arisen.

It is now high time that I should explain to your Excellencies the object of my voyage. Your Excellencies will bear in mind that distressed circumstances in Rotterdam had at length driven me to the resolution of committing suicide.

It was not, however, that to life itself I had any positive disgust, but that I was harassed beyond endurance by the adventitious miseries attending my situation. In this state of mind, wishing to live, yet wearied with life, the treatise at the stall of the bookseller, backed by the opportune discovery of my cousin of Nantz, opened a resource to my imagination. I then finally made up my mind. I determined to depart, yet live — to leave the world, yet continue to exist — in short, to drop enigmas, I resolved, let what would ensue, to force a passage, if I could, to the moon. Now, lest I should be supposed more of a madman than I actually am, I will detail, as well as I am able, the considerations which led me to believe that an achievement of this nature, although without doubt difficult, and full of danger, was not absolutely, to a bold spirit, beyond the confines of the possible.

The moon's actual distance from the earth was the first thing to be attended to. Now, the mean or average interval between the centres of the two planets is 59.9643 of the earth's equatorial radii, or only about 237,000 miles. I say the mean or average interval; — but it must be borne in mind, that the form of the moon's orbit being an ellipse of eccentricity amounting to no less than 0.05484 of the major semi-axis of the ellipse itself, and the earth's centre being situated in its focus, if I could, in any manner, contrive to meet the moon in its perigee, the above-mentioned distance would be materially diminished. But to say nothing, at present, of this possibility, it was very certain that, at all events, from the 237,000 miles I would have to deduct the radius of the earth, say 4000, and the radius of the moon, say 1080, in all 5080, leaving an actual interval to be traversed, under average circumstances, of 231,920 miles. Now this, I reflected, was no very extraordinary distance. Travelling on the land has been repeatedly accomplished at the rate of sixty miles per hour; and indeed a much greater speed may be anticipated. But even at this velocity, it would take me no more than 161 days to reach the surface of the moon. There were, however, many particulars inducing me to believe that my average rate of travelling might possibly very much exceed that of sixty miles per hour, and, as these considerations did not fail to make a deep impression upon my mind, I will mention them more fully hereafter.

The next point to be regarded was one of far greater importance. From indications afforded by the barometer, we find that, in ascensions from the surface of the earth we have, at the height of a 1000 feet, left below us about one-thirtieth of the entire mass of atmospheric air; that at 10,600, we have ascended through nearly one-third; and that at 18,000, which is not far from the elevation of Cotopaxi, we have surmounted one-half the material, or, at all events, one-half the ponderable body of air incumbent upon our globe. It is also calculated, that at an altitude not exceeding the hundredth part of the earth's diameter — that is, not exceeding eighty miles — the rarefaction would be so excessive that animal life could in no manner be sustained, and, moreover, that the most delicate means we possess of ascertaining the presence of the atmosphere, would be inadequate to assure us of its existence. But I did not fail to perceive that these latter calculations are founded altogether on our experimental knowledge of the properties of air, and the mechanical laws regulating its dilation and compression, in what may be called, comparatively speaking, the immediate vicinity of the earth itself; and, at the same time, it is taken for granted that animal life is and must be, essentially incapable of modification at any given unattainable distance from the surface. Now, all such reasoning and from such data, must of course be simply analogical. The greatest height ever reached by man was that of 25,000 feet, attained in the æronautic expedition of Messieurs Gay-Lussac and Biot. This is a moderate altitude, even when compared with the eighty miles in question; and I could not help thinking that the subject admitted room for doubt, and great latitude for speculation.

But, in point of fact, an ascension being made to any given altitude, the ponderable quantity of air surmounted in any farther ascension, is by no means in proportion to the additional height ascended, (as may be plainly seen from what has been stated before,) but in a ratio constantly decreasing. It is therefore evident that, ascend as high as we may, we cannot, literally speaking, arrive at a limit beyond which no atmosphere is to be found. It must exist, I argued; although it may exist in a state of infinite rarefaction.

On the other hand, I was aware that arguments have not been wanting to prove the existence of a real and definite limit to the atmosphere, beyond which there is absolutely no air whatsoever. But a circumstance which has been left out of view by those who contend for such a limit, seemed to me, although no positive refutation of their creed, still a point worthy very serious investigation. On comparing the intervals between the successive arrivals of Encke's comet at its perihelion, after giving credit, in the most exact manner, for all the disturbances due to the attractions of the planets, it appears that the periods are gradually diminishing; that is to say, the major axis of the comet's ellipse is growing shorter, in a slow but perfectly regular decrease. Now, this is precisely what ought to be the case, if we suppose a resistance experienced from the comet from an extremely rare ethereal medium pervading the regions of its orbit. For it is evident that such a medium must, in retarding the comet's velocity, increase its centripetal, by weakening its centrifugal force. In other words, the sun's attraction would be constantly attaining greater power, and the comet would be drawn nearer at every revolution. Indeed, there is no other way of accounting for the variation in question. But again: — The real diameter of the same comet's nebulosity, is observed to contract rapidly as it approaches the sun, and dilate with equal rapidity in its departure toward its aphelion. Was I not justifiable in supposing, with M. Valz, that this apparent condensation of volume has its origin in the compression of the same ethereal medium I have spoken of before, and which is dense in proportion to its vicinity to the sun? The lenticular-shaped phenomenon, also, called the zodiacal light, was a matter worthy of attention. This radiance, so apparent in the tropics, and which cannot be mistaken for any meteoric lustre, extends from the horizon obliquely upwards, and follows generally the direction of the sun's equator. It appeared to me evidently in the nature of a rare atmosphere extending from the sun outwards, beyond the orbit of Venus at least, and I believed indefinitely farther.* Indeed, this medium I could not suppose confined to the path of the comet's ellipse, or to the immediate neighborhood of the sun. It was easy, on the contrary, to imagine it pervading the entire regions of our planetary system, condensed into what we call atmosphere at the planets themselves, and perhaps at some of them modified by considerations purely geological; that is to say, modified, or varied in its proportions (or absolute nature) by matters volatilized from the respective orbs.

Having adopted this view of the subject, I had little farther hesitation. Granting that on my passage I should meet with atmosphere essentially the same as at the surface of the earth, I conceived that, by means of the very ingenious apparatus of M. Grimm, I should readily be enabled to condense it in sufficient quantity for the purposes of respiration. This would remove the chief obstacle in a journey to the moon. I had indeed spent some money and great labor in adapting the apparatus to the object intended, and confidently looked forward to its successful application, if I could manage to complete the voyage within any reasonable period. — This brings me back to the rate at which it would be possible to travel.

It is true that balloons, in the first stage of their ascensions from the earth, are known to rise with a velocity comparatively moderate. Now, the power of elevation lies altogether in the superior gravity of the atmospheric air compared with the gas in the balloon; and, at first sight, it does not appear probable that, as the balloon acquires altitude, and consequently arrives successively in atmospheric strata of densities rapidly diminishing — I say, it does not appear at all reasonable that, in this its progress upward, the original velocity should be accelerated. On the other hand, I was not aware that, in any recorded ascension, a diminution had been proved to be apparent in the absolute rate of ascent; although such should have been the case, if on account of nothing else, on account of the escape of gas through balloons ill-constructed, and varnished with no better material than the ordinary varnish. It seemed, therefore, that the effect of such escape was only sufficient to counterbalance the effect of the acceleration attained in the diminishing of the balloon's distance from the gravitating centre. I now considered that, provided in my passage I found the medium I had imagined, and provided it should prove to be essentially what we denominate atmospheric air, it could make comparatively little difference at what extreme state of rarefaction I should discover it — that is to say, in regard to my power of ascending — for the gas in the balloon would not only be itself subject to similar rarefaction, (in proportion to the occurrence of which, I could suffer an escape of so much as would be requisite to prevent explosion,) but, being what it was, would, at all events, continue specifically lighter than any compound whatever of mere nitrogen and oxygen. Thus there was a chance — in fact, there was a strong probability — that, at no epoch of my ascent, I should reach a point where the united weights of my immense balloon, the inconceivably rare gas within it, the car, and its contents, should equal the weight of the mass of the surrounding atmosphere displaced; and this will be readily understood as the sole condition upon which my upward flight would be arrested. But, if this point were even attained, I could dispense with ballast and other weight to the amount of nearly 300 pounds. In the meantime, the force of gravitation would be constantly diminishing, in proportion to the squares of the distances, and so, with a velocity prodigiously accelerating, I should at length arrive in those distant regions where the force of the earth's attraction would be superseded by that of the moon.

There was another difficulty, however, which occasioned me some little disquietude. It has been observed, that, in balloon ascensions to any considerable height, besides the pain attending respiration, great uneasiness is experienced about the head and body, often accompanied with bleeding at the nose, and other symptoms of an alarming kind, and growing more and more inconvenient in proportion to the altitude attained.* This was a reflection of a nature somewhat startling. Was it not probable that these symptoms would increase until terminated by death itself? I finally thought not. Their origin was to be looked for in the progressive removal of the customary atmospheric pressure upon the surface of the body, and consequent distention of the superficial blood-vessels — not in any positive disorganization of the animal system, as in the case of difficulty in breathing, where the atmospheric density is chemically insufficient for the due renovation of blood in a ventricle of the heart. Unless for default of this renovation, I could see no reason, therefore, why life could not be sustained even in a vacuum; for the expansion and compression of chest, commonly called breathing, is action purely muscular, and the cause, not the effect, of respiration. In a word, I conceived that, as the body should become habituated to the want of atmospheric pressure, these sensations of pain would gradually diminish — and to endure them while they continued, I relied with confidence upon the iron hardihood of my constitution. Thus, may it please your Excellencies, I have detailed some, though by no means all, the considerations which led me to form the project of a lunar voyage. I shall now proceed to lay before you the result of an attempt so apparently audacious in conception, and, at all events, so utterly unparalleled in the annals of mankind.

Having attained the altitude before mentioned — that is to say, three miles and three quarters — I threw out from the car a quantity of feathers, and found that I still ascended with sufficient rapidity; there was, therefore, no necessity for discharging any ballast. I was glad of this, for I wished to retain with me as much weight as I could carry, for the obvious reason that I could not be positive either about the gravitation or the atmospheric density of the moon. I as yet suffered no bodily inconvenience, breathing with great freedom, and feeling no pain whatever in the head. The cat was lying very demurely upon my coat, which I had taken off, and eyeing the pigeons with an air of nonchalance. These latter being tied by the leg, to prevent their escape, were busily employed in picking up some grains of rice scattered for them in the bottom of the car.

At twenty minutes past six o'clock, the barometer showed an elevation of 26,400 feet, or five miles to a fraction. The prospect seemed unbounded. Indeed, it is very easily calculated by means of spherical geometry, how great an extent of the earth's area I beheld. The convex surface of any segment of a sphere is, to the entire surface of the sphere itself, as the versed sine of the segment to the diameter of the sphere. Now, in my case, the versed sine — that is to say, the thickness of the segment beneath me — was about equal to my elevation, or the elevation of the point of sight above the surface. "As five miles, then, to eight thousand," would express the proportion of the earth's area seen by me. In other words, I beheld as much as a sixteen-hundredth part of the whole surface of the globe. The sea appeared unruffled as a mirror, although, by means of the telescope, I could perceive it to be in a state of violent agitation. The ship was no longer visible, having drifted away, apparently, to the eastward. I now began to experience, at intervals, severe pain in the head, especially about the ears — still, however, breathing with tolerable freedom. The cat and pigeons seemed to suffer no inconvenience whatsoever.

At twenty minutes before seven, the balloon entered a

long series of dense cloud, which put me to great trouble, by damaging my condensing apparatus, and wetting me to the skin. This was, to be sure, a singular rencontre, for I had not believed it possible that a cloud of this nature could be sustained at so great an elevation. I thought it best, however, to throw out two five-pound pieces of ballast, reserving still a weight of one hundred and sixty-five pounds. Upon so doing, I soon rose above the difficulty, and perceived immediately, that I had obtained a great increase in my rate of ascent. In a few seconds after my leaving the cloud, a flash of vivid lightning shot from one end of it to the other, and caused it to kindle up, throughout its vast extent, like a mass of ignited charcoal. This, it must be remembered, was in the broad light of day. No fancy may picture the sublimity which might have been exhibited by a similar phenomenon taking place amid the darkness of the night. Hell itself might then have found a fitting image. Even as it was, my hair stood on end, while I gazed afar down within the yawning abysses, letting imagination descend, and stalk about in the strange vaulted halls, and ruddy gulfs, and red ghastly chasms of the hideous and unfathomable fire. I had indeed made a narrow escape. Had the balloon remained a very short while longer within the cloud — that is to say, had not the inconvenience of getting wet, determined me to discharge the ballast — my destruction might, and probably would, have been the consequence. Such perils, although little considered, are perhaps the greatest which must be encountered in balloons. I had by this time, however, attained too great an elevation to be any longer uneasy on this head.

I was now rising rapidly, and by seven o'clock the barometer indicated an altitude of no less than nine miles and a half. I began to find great difficulty in drawing my breath. My head, too, was excessively painful; and, having felt for some time a moisture about my cheeks, I at length discovered it to be blood, which was oozing quite fast from the drums of my ears. My eyes, also, gave me great uneasiness. Upon passing the hand over them they seemed to have protruded from their sockets in no inconsiderable degree; and all objects in the car, and even the balloon itself, appeared distorted to my vision. These symptoms were more than I had expected, and occasioned me some alarm. At this juncture, very imprudently, and without consideration, I threw out from the car three five-pound pieces of ballast. The accelerated rate of ascent thus obtained, carried me too rapidly, and without sufficient gradation, into a highly rarefied stratum of the atmosphere, and the result had nearly proved fatal to my expedition and to myself. I was suddenly seized with a spasm which lasted for more than five minutes, and even when this, in a measure, ceased, I could catch my breath only at long intervals, and in a gasping manner, — bleeding all the while copiously at the nose and ears, and even slightly at the eyes. The pigeons appeared distressed in the extreme, and struggled to escape; while the cat mewed piteously, and, with her tongue hanging out of her mouth, staggered to and fro in the car as if under the influence of poison. I now too late discovered the great rashness of which I had been guilty in discharging the ballast, and my agitation was excessive. I anticipated nothing less than death, and death in a few minutes. The physical suffering I underwent contributed also to render me nearly incapable of making any exertion for the preservation of my life. I had, indeed, little power of reflection left, and the violence of the pain in my head seemed to be greatly on the increase. Thus I found that my senses would shortly give way altogether, and I had already clutched one of the valve ropes with the view of attempting a descent, when the recollection of the trick I had played the three creditors, and the possible consequences to myself, should I return, operated to deter me for the moment. I lay down in the bottom of the car, and endeavored to collect my faculties. In this I so far succeeded as to determine upon the experiment of losing blood. Having no lancet, however, I was constrained to perform the operation in the best manner I was able, and finally succeeded in opening a vein in my left arm, with the blade of my penknife. The blood had hardly commenced flowing when I experienced a sensible relief, and by the time I had lost about half a moderate basin-full, most of the worst symptoms had abandoned me entirely. I nevertheless did not think it expedient to attempt getting on my feet immediately; but, having tied up my arm as well as I could, I lay still for about a quarter of an hour. At the end of this time I arose, and found myself freer from absolute pain of any kind than I had been during the last hour and a quarter of my ascension. The difficulty of breathing, however, was diminished in a very slight degree, and I found that it would soon be positively necessary to make use of my condenser. In the meantime, looking towards the cat, who was again snugly stowed away upon my coat, I discovered, to my infinite surprise, that she had taken the opportunity of my indisposition to bring into light a litter of three little kittens. This was an addition to the number of passengers on my part altogether unexpected; but I was pleased at the occurrence. It would afford me a chance of bringing to a kind of test the truth of a surmise, which, more than any thing else, had influenced me in attempting this ascension. I had imagined that the habitual endurance of the atmospheric pressure at the surface of the earth was the cause, or nearly so, of the pain attending animal existence at a distance above the surface. Should the kittens be found to suffer uneasiness in an equal degree with their mother, I must consider my theory in fault, but a failure to do so I should look upon as a strong confirmation of my idea.

By eight o'clock I had actually attained an elevation of seventeen miles above the surface of the earth. Thus it seemed to me evident that my rate of ascent was not only on the increase, but that the progression would have been apparent in a slight degree even had I not discharged the ballast which I did. The pains in my head and ears returned, at intervals, with violence, and I still continued to bleed occasionally at the nose: but, upon the whole, I suffered much less than might have been expected. I breathed, however, at every moment, with more and more difficulty, and each inhalation was attended with a troublesome spasmodic action of the chest. I now unpacked the condensing apparatus, and got it ready for immediate use.

The view of the earth, at this period of my ascension, was beautiful indeed. To the westward, the northward, and the southward, as far as I could see, lay a boundless sheet of apparently unruffled ocean, which every moment gained a deeper and deeper tint of blue. At a vast distance to the eastward, although perfectly discernible, extended the islands of Great Britain, the entire Atlantic coasts of France and Spain, with a small portion of the northern part of the continent of Africa. Of individual edifices not a trace could be discovered, and the proudest cities of mankind had utterly faded away from the face of the earth.

What mainly astonished me, in the appearance of things below, was the seeming concavity of the surface of the globe. I had, thoughtlessly enough, expected to see its real convexity become evident as I ascended; but a very little reflection sufficed to explain the discrepancy. A line, dropped from my position perpendicularly to the earth, would have formed the perpendicular of a right-angled triangle, of which the base would have extended from the right-angle to the horizon, and the hypothenuse from the horizon to my position. But my height was little or nothing in comparison with my prospect. In other words, the base and hypothenuse of the supposed triangle would, in my case, have been so long, when compared to the perpendicular, that the two former might have been regarded as nearly parallel. In this manner the horizon of the æronaut appears always to be upon a level with the car. But as the point immediately beneath him seems, and is, at a great distance below him, it seems, of course, also at a great distance below the horizon. Hence the impression of concavity; and this impression must remain, until the elevation shall bear so great a proportion to the prospect, that the apparent parallelism of the base and hypothenuse, disappears.

The pigeons about this time seeming to undergo much suffering, I determined upon giving them their liberty. I first untied one of them, a beautiful gray-mottled pigeon, and placed him upon the rim of the wicker-work. He appeared extremely uneasy, looking anxiously around him, fluttering his wings, and making a loud cooing noise, but could not be persuaded to trust himself from the car. I took him up at last, and threw him to about half-a-dozen yards from the balloon. He made, however, no attempt to descend as I had expected, but struggled with great vehemence to get back, uttering at the same time very shrill and piercing cries. He at length succeeded in regaining his former station on the rim, but had hardly done so when his head dropped upon his breast, and he fell dead within the car. The other one did not prove so unfortunate. To prevent his following the example of his companion, and accomplishing a return, I threw him downwards with all my force, and was pleased to find him continue his descent, with great velocity, making use of his wings with ease, and in a perfectly natural manner. In a very short time he was out of sight, and I have no doubt he reached home in safety. Puss, who seemed in a great measure recovered from her illness, now made a hearty meal of the dead bird, and then went to sleep with much apparent satisfaction. Her kittens were quite lively, and so far evinced not the slightest sign of any uneasiness.

At a quarter-past eight, being able no longer to draw breath without the most intolerable pain, I proceeded, forthwith, to adjust around the car the apparatus belonging to the condenser. This apparatus will require some little explanation, and your Excellencies will please to bear in mind that my object, in the first place, was to surround myself and car entirely with a barricade against the highly rarefied atmosphere in which I was existing, with the intention of introducing within this barricade, by means of my condenser, a quantity of this same atmosphere sufficiently condensed for the purposes of respiration. With this object in view I had prepared a very strong, perfectly air-tight, but flexible gum-elastic bag. In this bag, which was of sufficient dimensions, the entire car was in a manner placed. That is to say, it (the bag) was drawn over the whole bottom of the car, up its sides, and so on, along the outside of the ropes, to the upper rim or hoop where the net-work is attached. Having pulled the bag up in this way, and formed a complete enclosure on all sides, and at bottom, it was now necessary to fasten up its top or mouth, by passing its material over the hoop of the net-work, — in other words, between the net-work and the hoop. But if the net-work were separated from the hoop to admit this passage, what was to sustain the car in the meantime? Now the net-work was not permanently fastened to the hoop, but attached by a series of running loops or nooses. I therefore undid only a few of these loops at one time, leaving the car suspended by the remainder. Having thus inserted a portion of the cloth forming the upper part of the bag, I refastened the loops — not to the hoop, for that would have been impossible, since the cloth now intervened, — but to a series of large buttons, affixed to the cloth itself, about three feet below the mouth of the bag; the intervals between the buttons having been made to correspond to the intervals between the loops. This done, a few more of the loops were unfastened from the rim, a farther portion of the cloth introduced, and the disengaged loops then connected with their proper buttons. In this way it was possible to insert the whole upper part of the bag between the net-work and the hoop. It is evident that the hoop would now drop down within the car, while the whole weight of the car itself, with all its contents, would be held up merely by the strength of the buttons. This, at first sight, would seem an inadequate dependence; but it was by no means so, for the buttons were not only very strong in themselves, but so close together that a very slight portion of the whole weight was supported by any one of them. Indeed, had the car and contents been three times heavier than they were, I should not have been at all uneasy. I now raised up the hoop again within the covering of gum-elastic, and propped it at nearly its former height by means of three light poles prepared for the occasion. This was done, of course, to keep the bag distended at the top, and to preserve the lower part of the net-work in its proper situation. All that now remained was to fasten up the mouth of the enclosure; and this was readily accomplished by gathering the folds of the material together, and twisting them up very tightly on the inside by means of a kind of stationary tourniquet.

In the sides of the covering thus adjusted round the car, had been inserted three circular panes of thick but clear glass, through which I could see without difficulty around me in every horizontal direction. In that portion of the cloth forming the bottom, was likewise a fourth window, of the same kind, and corresponding with a small aperture in the floor of the car itself. This enabled me to see perpendicularly down, but having found it impossible to place any similar contrivance overhead, on account of the peculiar manner of closing up the opening there, and the consequent wrinkles in the cloth, I could expect to see no objects situated directly in my zenith. This, of course, was a matter of little consequence; for, had I even been able to place a window at top, the balloon itself would have prevented my making any use of it.

About a foot below one of the side windows was a circular opening, three inches in diameter, and fitted with a brass rim adapted in its inner edge to the windings of a screw. In this rim was screwed the large tube of the condenser, the body of the machine being, of course, within the chamber of gum-elastic. Through this tube a quantity of the rare atmosphere circumjacent being drawn by means of a vacuum created in the body of the machine, was thence discharged, in a state of condensation, to mingle with the thin air already in the chamber. This operation, being repeated several times, at length filled the chamber with atmosphere proper for all the purposes of respiration. But in so confined a space it would, in a short time, necessarily become foul, and unfit for use from frequent contact with the lungs. It was then ejected by a small valve at the bottom of the car; — the dense air readily sinking into the thinner atmosphere below. To avoid the inconvenience of making a total vacuum at any moment within the chamber, this purification was never accomplished all at once, but in a gradual manner, — the valve being opened only for a few seconds, then closed again, until one or two strokes from the pump of the condenser had supplied the place of the atmosphere ejected. For the sake of experiment I had put the cat and kittens in a small basket, and suspended it outside the car to a button at the bottom, close by the valve, through which I could feed them at any moment when necessary. I did this at some little risk, and before closing the mouth of the chamber, by reaching under the car with one of the poles before mentioned to which a hook had been attached. As soon as dense air was admitted in the chamber, the hoop and poles became unnecessary; the expansion of the enclosed atmosphere powerfully distending the gum-elastic.

By the time I had fully completed these arrangements and filled the chamber as explained, it wanted only ten minutes of nine o'clock. During the whole period of my being thus employed, I endured the most terrible distress from difficulty of respiration; and bitterly did I repent the negligence, or rather fool-hardiness, of which I had been guilty, of putting off to the last moment a matter of so much importance. But having at length accomplished it, I soon began to reap the benefit of my invention. Once again I breathed with perfect freedom and ease — and indeed why should I not? I was also agreeably surprised to find myself, in a great measure, relieved from the violent pains which had hitherto tormented me. A slight headache, accompanied with a sensation of fulness or distention about the wrists, the ankles, and the throat, was nearly all of which I had now to complain. Thus it seemed evident that a greater part of the uneasiness attending the removal of atmospheric pressure had actually worn off, as I had expected, and that much of the pain endured for the last two hours should have been attributed altogether to the effects of a deficient respiration.

At twenty minutes before nine o'clock — that is to say, a short time prior to my closing up the mouth of the chamber, the mercury attained its limit, or ran down, in the barometer, which, as I mentioned before, was one of an extended construction. It then indicated an altitude on my part of 132,000 feet, or five-and-twenty miles, and I consequently surveyed at that time an extent of the earth's area amounting to no less than the three-hundred-and-twentieth part of its entire superficies. At nine o'clock I had again lost sight of land to the eastward, but not before I became aware that the balloon was drifting rapidly to the N. N. W. The ocean beneath me still retained its apparent concavity, although my view was often interrupted by the masses of cloud which floated to and fro.

At half past nine I tried the experiment of throwing out a handful of feathers through the valve. They did not float as I had expected; but dropped down perpendicularly, like a bullet, en masse, and with the greatest velocity, — being out of sight in a very few seconds. I did not at first know what to make of this extraordinary phenomenon; not being able to believe that my rate of ascent had, of a sudden, met with so prodigious an acceleration. But it soon occurred to me that the atmosphere was now far too rare to sustain even the feathers; that they actually fell, as they appeared to do, with great rapidity; and that I had been surprised by the united velocities of their descent and my own elevation.

By ten o'clock I found that I had very little to occupy my immediate attention. Affairs went on swimmingly, and I believed the balloon to be going upwards with a speed increasing momently, although I had no longer any means of ascertaining the progression of the increase. I suffered no pain or uneasiness of any kind, and enjoyed better spirits than I had at any period since my departure from Rotterdam; busying myself now in examining the state of my various apparatus, and now in regenerating the atmosphere within the chamber. This latter point I determined to attend to at regular intervals of forty minutes, more on account of the preservation of my health, than from so frequent a renovation being absolutely necessary. In the meanwhile I could not help making anticipations. Fancy revelled in the wild and dreamy regions of the moon. Imagination, feeling herself for once unshackled, roamed at will among the ever-changing wonders of a shadowy and unstable land. Now there were hoary and time-honored forests, and craggy precipices, and waterfalls tumbling with a loud noise into abysses without a bottom. Then I came suddenly into still noonday solitudes, where no wind of heaven ever intruded, and where vast meadows of poppies, and slender, lily-looking flowers spread themselves out a weary distance, all silent and motionless for ever. Then again I journeyed far down away into another country where it was all one dim and vague lake, with a boundary-line of clouds. But fancies such as these were not the sole possessors of my brain. Horrors of a nature most stern and most appalling would too frequently obtrude themselves upon my mind, and shake the innermost depths of my soul with the bare supposition of their possibility. Yet I would not suffer my thoughts for any length of time to dwell upon these latter speculations, rightly judging the real and palpable dangers of the voyage sufficient for my undivided attention.

At five o'clock, P. M., being engaged in regenerating the atmosphere within the chamber, I took that opportunity of observing the cat and kittens through the valve. The cat herself appeared to suffer again very much, and I had no hesitation in attributing her uneasiness chiefly to a difficulty in breathing; but my experiment with the kittens had resulted very strangely. I had expected, of course, to see them betray a sense of pain, although in a less degree than their mother; and this would have been sufficient to confirm my opinion concerning the habitual endurance of atmospheric pressure. But I was not prepared to find them, upon close examination, evidently enjoying a high degree of health, breathing with the greatest ease and perfect regularity, and evincing not the slightest sign of any uneasiness. I could only account for all this by extending my theory, and supposing that the highly rarefied atmosphere around, might perhaps not be, as I had taken for granted, chemically insufficient for the purposes of life, and that a person born in such a medium might, possibly, be unaware of any inconvenience attending its inhalation, while, upon removal to the denser strata near the earth, he might endure tortures of a similar nature to those I had so lately experienced. It has since been to me a matter of deep regret that an awkward accident, at this time, occasioned me the loss of my little family of cats, and deprived me of the insight into this matter which a continued experiment might have afforded. In passing my hand through the valve, with a cup of water for the old puss, the sleeve of my shirt became entangled in the loop which sustained the basket, and thus, in a moment, loosened it from the button. Had the whole actually vanished into air, it could not have shot from my sight in a more abrupt and instantaneous manner. Positively, there could not have intervened the tenth part of a second between the disengagement of the basket and its absolute disappearance with all that it contained. My good wishes followed it to the earth, but, of course, I had no hope that either cat or kittens would ever live to tell the tale of their misfortune.

At six o'clock, I perceived a great portion of the earth's visible area to the eastward involved in thick shadow, which continued to advance with great rapidity, until, at five minutes before seven, the whole surface in view was enveloped in the darkness of night. It was not, however, until long after this time that the rays of the setting sun ceased to illumine the balloon; and this circumstance, although of course fully anticipated, did not fail to give me an infinite deal of pleasure. It was evident that, in the morning, I should behold the rising luminary many hours at least before the citizens of Rotterdam, in spite of their situation so much farther to the eastward, and thus, day after day, in proportion to the height ascended, would I enjoy the light of the sun for a longer and a longer period. I now determined to keep a journal of my passage, reckoning the days from one to twenty-four hours continuously, without taking into consideration the intervals of darkness.

At ten o'clock, feeling sleepy, I determined to lie down for the rest of the night; but here a difficulty presented itself, which, obvious as it may appear, had escaped my attention up to the very moment of which I am now speaking. If I went to sleep as I proposed, how could the atmosphere in the chamber be regenerated in the interim? To breathe it for more than an hour, at the farthest, would be a matter of impossibility; or, if even this term could be extended to an hour and a quarter, the most ruinous consequences might ensue. The consideration of this dilemma gave me no little disquietude; and it will hardly be believed, that, after the dangers I had undergone, I should look upon this business in so serious a light, as to give up all hope of accomplishing my ultimate design, and finally make up my mind to the necessity of a descent. But this hesitation was only momentary. I reflected that man is the veriest slave of custom, and that many points in the routine of his existence are deemed essentially important, which are only so at all by his having rendered them habitual. It was very certain that I could not do without sleep; but I might easily bring myself to feel no inconvenience from being awakened at intervals of an hour during the whole period of my repose. It would require but five minutes at most, to regenerate the atmosphere in the fullest manner — and the only real difficulty was, to contrive a method of arousing myself at the proper moment for so doing. But this was a question which, I am willing to confess, occasioned me no little trouble in its solution. To be sure, I had heard of the student who, to prevent his falling asleep over his books, held in one hand a ball of copper, the din of whose descent into a basin of the same metal on the floor beside his chair, served effectually to startle him up, if, at any moment, he should be overcome with drowsiness. My own case, however, was very different indeed, and left me no room for any similar idea; for I did not wish to keep awake, but to be aroused from slumber at regular intervals of time. I at length hit upon the following expedient, which, simple as it may seem, was hailed by me, at the moment of discovery, as an invention fully equal to that of the telescope, the steam-engine, or the art of printing itself.

It is necessary to premise, that the balloon, at the elevation now attained, continued its course upwards with an even and undeviating ascent, and the car consequently followed with a steadiness so perfect that it would have been impossible to detect in it the slightest vacillation. This circumstance favored me greatly in the project I now determined to adopt. My supply of water had been put on board in kegs containing five gallons each, and ranged very securely around the interior of the car. I unfastened one of these, and taking two ropes, tied them tightly across the rim of the wicker-work from one side to the other; placing them about a foot apart and parallel, so as to form a kind of shelf, upon which I placed the keg, and steadied it in a horizontal position. About eight inches immediately below these ropes, and four feet from the bottom of the car, I fastened another shelf — but made of thin plank, being the only similar piece of wood I had. Upon this latter shelf, and exactly beneath one of the rims of the keg, a small earthen pitcher was deposited. I now bored a hole in the end of the keg over the pitcher, and fitted in a plug of soft wood, cut in a tapering or conical shape. This plug I pushed in or pulled out, as might happen, until, after a few experiments, It arrived at that exact degree of tightness, at which the water, oozing from the hole, and falling into the pitcher below, would fill the latter to the brim in the period of sixty minutes. This, of course, was a matter briefly and easily ascertained, by noticing the proportion of the pitcher filled in any given time. Having arranged all this, the rest of the plan is obvious. My bed was so contrived upon the floor of the car, as to bring my head, in lying down, immediately below the mouth of the pitcher. It was evident, that, at the expiration of an hour, the pitcher, getting full, would be forced to run over, and to run over at the mouth, which was somewhat lower than the rim. It was also evident, that the water, thus falling from a height of more than four feet, could not do otherwise than fall upon my face, and that the sure consequence would be, to waken me up instantaneously, even from the soundest slumber in the world.

It was fully eleven by the time I had completed these arrangements, and I immediately betook myself to bed, with full confidence in the efficiency of my invention. Nor in this matter was I disappointed. Punctually every sixty minutes was I aroused by my trusty chronometer, when, having emptied the pitcher into the bung-hole of the keg, and performed the duties of the condenser, I retired again to bed. These regular interruptions to my slumber caused me even less discomfort than I had anticipated; and when I finally arose for the day, it was seven o'clock, and the sun had attained many degrees above the line of my horizon.

April 3d. I found the balloon at an immense height indeed, and the earth's convexity had now become strikingly manifest. Below me in the ocean lay a cluster of black specks, which undoubtedly were islands. Overhead, the sky was of a jetty black, and the stars were brilliantly visible; indeed they had been so constantly since the first day of ascent. Far away to the northward I perceived a thin, white, and exceedingly brilliant line, or streak, on the edge of the horizon, and I had no hesitation in supposing it to be the southern disc of the ices of the Polar sea. My curiosity was greatly excited, for I had hopes of passing on much farther to the north, and might possibly, at some period, find myself placed directly above the Pole itself. I now lamented that my great elevation would, in this case, prevent my taking as accurate a survey as I could wish. Much, however, might be ascertained.

Nothing else of an extraordinary nature occurred during the day. My apparatus all continued in good order, and the balloon still ascended without any perceptible vacillation. The cold was intense, and obliged me to wrap up closely in an overcoat. When darkness came over the earth, I betook myself to bed, although it was for many hours afterwards broad daylight all around my immediate situation. The water-clock was punctual in its duty, and I slept until next morning soundly, with the exception of the periodical interruption.

April 4th. Arose in good health and spirits, and was astonished at the singular change which had taken place in the appearance of the sea. It had lost, in a great measure, the deep tint of blue it had hitherto worn, being now of a grayish-white, and of a lustre dazzling to the eye. The convexity of the ocean had become so evident, that the entire mass of the distant water seemed to be tumbling headlong over the abyss of the horizon, and I found myself listening on tiptoe for the echoes of the mighty cataract. The islands were no longer visible; whether they had passed down the horizon to the south-east, or whether my increasing elevation had left them out of sight, it is impossible to say. I was inclined, however, to the latter opinion. The rim of ice to the northward was growing more and more apparent. Cold by no means so intense. Nothing of importance occurred, and I passed the day in reading, having taken care to supply myself with books.

April 5th. Beheld the singular phenomenon of the sun rising while nearly the whole visible surface of the earth continued to be involved in darkness. In time, however, the light spread itself over all, and I again saw the line of ice to the northward. It was now very distinct, and appeared of a much darker hue than the waters of the ocean. I was evidently approaching it, and with great rapidity. Fancied I could again distinguish a strip of land to the eastward, and one also to the westward, but could not be certain. Weather moderate. Nothing of any consequence happened during the day. Went early to bed.

April 6th. Was surprised at finding the rim of ice at a very moderate distance, and an immense field of the same material stretching away off to the horizon in the north. It was evident that if the balloon held its present course, it would soon arrive above the Frozen Ocean, and I had now little doubt of ultimately seeing the Pole. During the whole of the day I continued to near the ice. Towards night the limits of my horizon very suddenly and materially increased, owing undoubtedly to the earth's form being that of an oblate spheroid, and my arriving above the flattened regions in the vicinity of the Arctic circle. When darkness at length overtook me, I went to bed in great anxiety, fearing to pass over the object of so much curiosity when I should have no opportunity of observing it.

April 7th. Arose early, and, to my great joy, at length beheld what there could be no hesitation in supposing the northern Pole itself. It was there, beyond a doubt, and immediately beneath my feet; but, alas! I had now ascended to so vast a distance, that nothing could with accuracy be discerned. Indeed, to judge from the progression of the numbers indicating my various altitudes, respectively, at different periods, between six, A. M., on the second of April, and twenty minutes before nine, A. M., of the same day, (at which time the barometer ran down,) it might be fairly inferred that the balloon had now, at four o'clock in the morning of April the seventh, reached a height of not less, certainly, than 7254 miles above the surface of the sea. This elevation may appear immense, but the estimate upon which it is calculated gave a result in all probability far inferior to the truth. At all events I undoubtedly beheld the whole of the earth's major diameter; the entire northern hemisphere lay beneath me like a chart orthographically projected; and the great circle of the equator itself formed the boundary line of my horizon. Your Excellencies may, however, readily imagine that the confined regions hitherto unexplored within the limits of the Arctic circle, although situated directly beneath me, and therefore seen without any appearance of being foreshortened, were still, in themselves, comparatively too diminutive, and at too great a distance from the point of sight, to admit of any very accurate examination. Nevertheless, what could be seen was of a nature singular and exciting. Northwardly from that huge rim before mentioned, and which, with slight qualification, may be called the limit of human discovery in these regions, one unbroken, or nearly unbroken sheet of ice continues to extend. In the first few degrees of this its progress, its surface is very sensibly flattened, farther on depressed into a plane, and finally, becoming not a little concave, it terminates, at the Pole itself, in a circular centre, sharply defined, whose apparent diameter subtended at the balloon an angle of about sixty-five seconds, and whose dusky hue, varying in intensity, was, at all times darker than any other spot upon the visible hemisphere, and occasionally deepened into the most absolute blackness. Farther than this, little could be ascertained. By twelve o'clock the circular centre had materially decreased in circumference, and by seven, P. M., I lost sight of it entirely; the balloon passing over the western limb of the ice, and floating away rapidly in the direction of the equator.

April 8th. Found a sensible diminution in the earth's apparent diameter, besides a material alteration in its general color and appearance. The whole visible area partook in different degrees of a tint of pale yellow, and in some portions had acquired a brilliancy even painful to the eye. My view downwards was also considerably impeded by the dense atmosphere in the vicinity of the surface being loaded with clouds, between whose masses I could only now and then obtain a glimpse of the earth itself. This difficulty of direct vision had troubled me more or less for the last forty-eight hours; but my present enormous elevation brought closer together, as it were, the floating bodies of vapor, and the inconvenience became, of course, more and more palpable in proportion to my ascent. Nevertheless, I could easily perceive that the balloon now hovered above the range of great lakes in the continent of North America, and was holding a course, due south, which would soon bring me to the tropics. This circumstance did not fail to give me the most heartfelt satisfaction, and I hailed it as a happy omen of ultimate success. Indeed, the direction I had hitherto taken, had filled me with uneasiness; for it was evident that, had I continued it much longer, there would have been no possibility of my arriving at the moon at all, whose orbit is inclined to the ecliptic at only the small angle of 5? 8' 48". Strange as it may seem, it was only at this late period that I began to understand the great error I had committed, in not taking my departure from earth at some point in the plane of the lunar ellipse.

April 9th. To-day, the earth's diameter was greatly diminished, and the color of the surface assumed hourly a deeper tint of yellow. The balloon kept steadily on her course to the southward, and arrived, at nine, P. M., over the northern edge of the Mexican Gulf.

April 10th. I was suddenly aroused from slumber, about five o'clock this morning, by a loud, crackling, and terrific sound, for which I could in no manner account. It was of very brief duration, but, while it lasted, resembled nothing in the world of which I had any previous experience. It is needless to say that I became excessively alarmed, having, in the first instance, attributed the noise to the bursting of the balloon. I examined all my apparatus, however, with great attention, and could discover nothing out of order. Spent a great part of the day in meditating upon an occurrence so extraordinary, but could find no means whatever of accounting for it. Went to bed dissatisfied, and in a state of great anxiety and agitation.

April 11th. Found a startling diminution in the apparent diameter of the earth, and a considerable increase, now observable for the first time, in that of the moon itself, which wanted only a few days of being full. It now required long and excessive labor to condense within the chamber sufficient atmospheric air for the sustenance of life.

April 12th. A singular alteration took place in regard to the direction of the balloon, and although fully anticipated, afforded me the most unequivocal delight. Having reached, in its former course, about the twentieth parallel of southern latitude, it turned off suddenly, at an acute angle, to the eastward, and thus proceeded throughout the day, keeping nearly, if not altogether, in the exact plane of the lunar ellipse. What was worthy of remark, a very perceptible vacillation in the car was a consequence of this change of route, — a vacillation which prevailed, in a more or less degree, for a period of many hours.

April 13th. Was again very much alarmed by a repetition of the loud crackling noise which terrified me on the tenth. Thought long upon the subject, but was unable to form any satisfactory conclusion. Great decrease in the earth's apparent diameter, which now subtended from the balloon an angle of very little more than twenty-five degrees. The moon could not be seen at all, being nearly in my zenith. I still continued in the plane of the ellipse, but made little progress to the eastward.

April 14th. Extremely rapid decrease in the diameter of the earth. To-day I became strongly impressed with the idea, that the balloon was now actually running up the line of apsides to the point of perigee, — in other words, holding the direct course which would bring it immediately to the moon in that part of its orbit the nearest to the earth. The moon itself was directly overhead, and consequently hidden from my view. Great and long continued labor necessary for the condensation of the atmosphere.

April 15th. Not even the outlines of continents and seas could now be traced upon the earth with distinctness. About twelve o'clock I became aware, for the third time, of that appalling sound which had so astonished me before. It now, however, continued for some moments, and gathered intensity as it continued. At length, while, stupified and terror-stricken, I stood in expectation of I knew not what hideous destruction, the car vibrated with excessive violence, and a gigantic and flaming mass of some material which I could not distinguish, came with a voice of a thousand thunders, roaring and booming by the balloon. When my fears and astonishment had in some degree subsided, I had little difficulty in supposing it to be some mighty volcanic fragment ejected from that world to which I was so rapidly approaching, and, in all probability, one of that singular class of substances occasionally picked up on the earth, and termed meteoric stones for want of a better appellation.

April 16th. To-day, looking upwards as well as I could, through each of the side windows alternately, I beheld, to my great delight, a very small portion of the moon's disk protruding, as it were, on all sides beyond the huge circumference of the balloon. My agitation was extreme; for I had now little doubt of soon reaching the end of my perilous voyage. Indeed, the labor now required by the condenser, had increased to a most oppressive degree, and allowed me scarcely any respite from exertion. Sleep was a matter nearly out of the question. I became quite ill, and my frame trembled with exhaustion. It was impossible that human nature could endure this state of intense suffering much longer. During the now brief interval of darkness a meteoric stone again passed in my vicinity, and the frequency of these phenomena began to occasion me much apprehension.

April 17th. This morning proved an epoch in my voyage. It will be remembered, that, on the thirteenth, the earth subtended an angular breadth of twenty-five degrees. On the fourteenth, this had greatly diminished; on the fifteenth, a still more rapid decrease was observable; and, on retiring for the night of the sixteenth, I had noticed an angle of no more than about seven degrees and fifteen minutes. What, therefore, must have been my amazement, on awakening from a brief and disturbed slumber, on the morning of this day, the seventeenth, at finding the surface beneath me so suddenly and wonderfully augmented in volume, as to subtend no less than thirty-nine degrees in apparent angular diameter! I was thunderstruck! No words can give any adequate idea of the extreme, the absolute horror and astonishment, with which I was seized, possessed, and altogether overwhelmed. My knees tottered beneath me — my teeth chattered — my hair started up on end. "The balloon, then, had actually burst!" These were the first tumultuous ideas which hurried through my mind: "The balloon had positively burst! — I was falling — falling with the most impetuous, the most unparalleled velocity! To judge from the immense distance already so quickly passed over, it could not be more than ten minutes, at the farthest, before I should meet the surface of the earth, and be hurled into annihilation!" But at length reflection came to my relief. I paused; I considered; and I began to doubt. The matter was impossible. I could not in any reason have so rapidly come down. Besides, although I was evidently approaching the surface below me, it was with a speed by no means commensurate with the velocity I had at first conceived. This consideration served to calm the perturbation of my mind, and I finally succeeded in regarding the phenomenon in its proper point of view. In fact, amazement must have fairly deprived me of my senses, when I could not see the vast difference, in appearance, between the surface below me, and the surface of my mother earth. The latter was indeed over my head, and completely hidden by the balloon, while the moon — the moon itself in all its glory — lay beneath me, and at my feet.

The stupor and surprise produced in my mind by this

extraordinary change in the posture of affairs, was perhaps, after all, that part of the adventure least susceptible of explanation. For the bouleversement in itself was not only natural and inevitable, but had been long actually anticipated, as a circumstance to be expected whenever I should arrive at that exact point of my voyage where the attraction of the planet should be superseded by the attraction of the satellite — or, more precisely, where the gravitation of the balloon towards the earth should be less powerful than its gravitation towards the moon. To be sure I arose from a sound slumber, with all my senses in confusion, to the contemplation of a very startling phenomenon, and one which, although expected, was not expected at the moment. The revolution itself must, of course, have taken place in an easy and gradual manner, and it is by no means clear that, had I even been awake at the time of the occurrence, I should have been made aware of it by any internal evidence of an inversion — that is to say, by any inconvenience or disarrangement, either about my person or about my apparatus.

It is almost needless to say, that, upon coming to a due sense of my situation, and emerging from the terror which had absorbed every faculty of my soul, my attention was, in the first place, wholly directed to the contemplation of the general physical appearance of the moon. It lay beneath me like a chart — and although I judged it to be still at no inconsiderable distance, the indentures of its surface were defined to my vision with a most striking and altogether unaccountable distinctness. The entire absence of ocean or sea, and indeed of any lake or river, or body of water whatsoever, struck me, at the first glance, as the most extraordinary feature in its geological condition. Yet, strange to say, I beheld vast level regions of a character decidedly alluvial, although by far the greater portion of the hemisphere in sight was covered with innumerable volcanic mountains, conical in shape, and having more the appearance of artificial than of natural protuberances. The highest among them does not exceed three and three-quarter miles in perpendicular elevation; but a map of the volcanic districts of the Campi Phlegræi would afford to your Excellencies a better idea of their general surface than any unworthy description I might think proper to attempt. The greater part of them were in a state of evident eruption, and gave me fearfully to understand their fury and their power, by the repeated thunders of the mis-called meteoric stones, which now rushed upwards by the balloon with a frequency more and more appalling.

April 18th. To-day I found an enormous increase in the moon's apparent bulk — and the evidently accelerated velocity of my descent, began to fill me with alarm. It will be remembered, that, in the earliest stage of my speculations upon the possibility of a passage to the moon, the existence, in its vicinity, of an atmosphere dense in proportion to the bulk of the planet, had entered largely into my calculations; this too in spite of many theories to the contrary, and, it may be added, in spite of a general disbelief in the existence of any lunar atmosphere at all. But, in addition to what I have already urged in regard to Encke's comet and the zodiacal light, I had been strengthened in my opinion by certain observations of Mr. Schroeter, of Lilienthal. He observed the moon, when two days and a half old, in the evening soon after sunset, before the dark part was visible, and continued to watch it until it became visible. The two cusps appeared tapering in a very sharp faint prolongation, each exhibiting its farthest extremity faintly illuminated by the solar rays, before any part of the dark hemisphere was visible. Soon afterwards, the whole dark limb became illuminated. This prolongation of the cusps beyond the semicircle, I thought, must have arisen from the refraction of the sun's rays by the moon's atmosphere. I computed, also, the height of the atmosphere (which could refract light enough into its dark hemisphere, to produce a twilight more luminous than the light reflected from the earth when the moon is about 32° from the new,) to be 1356 Paris feet; in this view, I supposed the greatest height capable of refracting the solar ray, to be 5376 feet. My ideas upon this topic had also received confirmation by a passage in the eighty-second volume of the Philosophical Transactions, in which it is stated, that, at an occultation of Jupiter's satellites, the third disappeared after having been about 1" or 2" of time indistinct, and the fourth became indiscernible near the limb.*

Upon the resistance, or more properly, upon the support of an atmosphere, existing in the state of density imagined, I had, of course, entirely depended for the safety of my ultimate descent. Should I then, after all, prove to have been mistaken, I had in consequence nothing better to expect, as a finale to my adventure, than being dashed into atoms against the rugged surface of the satellite. And, indeed, I had now every reason to be terrified. My distance from the moon was comparatively trifling, while the labor required by the condenser was diminished not at all, and I could discover no indication whatever of a decreasing rarity in the air.

April 19th. This morning, to my great joy, about nine o'clock, the surface of the moon being frightfully near, and my apprehensions excited to the utmost, the pump of my condenser at length gave evident tokens of an alteration in the atmosphere. By ten, I had reason to believe its density considerably increased. By eleven, very little labor was necessary at the apparatus; and at twelve o'clock, with some hesitation, I ventured to unscrew the tourniquet, when, finding no inconvenience from having done so, I finally threw open the gum-elastic chamber, and unrigged it from around the car. As might have been expected, spasms and violent headache were the immediate consequences of an experiment so precipitate and full of danger. But these and other difficulties attending respiration, as they were by no means so great as to put me in peril of my life, I determined to endure as I best could, in consideration of my leaving them behind me momently in my approach to the denser strata near the moon. This approach, however, was still impetuous in the extreme; and it soon became alarmingly certain that, although I had probably not been deceived in the expectation of an atmosphere dense in proportion to the mass of the satellite, still I had been wrong in supposing this density, even at the surface, at all adequate to the support of the great weight contained in the car of my balloon. Yet this should have been the case, and in an equal degree as at the surface of the earth, the actual gravity of bodies at either planet supposed in the ratio of the atmospheric condensation. That it was not the case, however, my precipitous downfall gave testimony enough; why it was not so, can only be explained by a reference to those possible geological disturbances to which I have formerly alluded. At all events I was now close upon the planet, and coming down with the most terrible impetuosity. I lost not a moment, accordingly, in throwing overboard first my ballast, then my water-kegs, then my condensing apparatus and gum-elastic chamber, and finally every article within the car. But it was all to no purpose. I still fell with horrible rapidity, and was now not more than half a mile from the surface. As a last resource, therefore, having got rid of my coat, hat, and boots, I cut loose from the balloon the car itself, which was of no inconsiderable weight, and thus, clinging with both hands to the net-work, I had barely time to observe that the whole country, as far as the eye could reach, was thickly interspersed with diminutive habitations, ere I tumbled headlong into the very heart of a fantastical-looking city, and into the middle of a vast crowd of ugly little people, who none of them uttered a single syllable, or gave themselves the least trouble to render me assistance, but stood, like a parcel of idiots, grinning in a ludicrous manner, and eyeing me and my balloon askant, with their arms set a-kimbo. I turned from them in contempt, and, gazing upwards at the earth so lately left, and left perhaps for ever, beheld it like a huge, dull, copper shield, about two degrees in diameter, fixed immovably in the heavens overhead, and tipped on one of its edges with a crescent border of the most brilliant gold. No traces of land or water could be discovered, and the whole was clouded with variable spots, and belted with tropical and equatorial zones.

Thus, may it please your Excellencies, after a series of great anxieties, unheard-of dangers, and unparalleled escapes, I had, at length, on the nineteenth day of my departure from Rotterdam, arrived in safety at the conclusion of a voyage undoubtedly the most extraordinary, and the most momentous, ever accomplished, undertaken, or conceived by any denizen of earth. But my adventures yet remain to be related. And indeed your Excellencies may well imagine that, after a residence of five years upon a planet not only deeply interesting in its own peculiar character, but rendered doubly so by its intimate connection, in capacity of satellite, with the world inhabited by man, I may have intelligence for the private ear of the States' College of Astronomers of far more importance than the details, however wonderful, of the mere voyage which so happily concluded. This is, in fact, the case. I have much — very much which it would give me the greatest pleasure to communicate. I have much to say of the climate of the planet; of its wonderful alternations of heat and cold; of unmitigated and burning sunshine for one fortnight, and more than polar frigidity for the next; of a constant transfer of moisture, by distillation like that in vacuo, from the point beneath the sun to the point the farthest from it; of a variable zone of running water; of the people themselves; of their manners, customs, and political institutions; of their peculiar physical construction; of their ugliness; of their want of ears, those useless appendages in an atmosphere so peculiarly modified; of their consequent ignorance of the use and properties of speech; of their substitute for speech in a singular method of inter-communication; of the incomprehensible connection between each particular individual in the moon, with some particular individual on the earth — a connection analogous with, and depending upon that of the orbs of the planet and the satellite, and by means of which the lives and destinies of the inhabitants of the one are interwoven with the lives and destinies of the inhabitants of the other; and above all, if it so please your Excellencies — above all of those dark and hideous mysteries which lie in the outer regions of the moon, — regions which, owing to the almost miraculous accordance of the satellite's rotation on its own axis with its sidereal revolution about the earth, have never yet been turned, and, by God's mercy, never shall be turned, to the scrutiny of the telescopes of man. All this, and more — much more — would I most willingly detail. But, to be brief, I must have my reward. I am pining for a return to my family and to my home: and as the price of any farther communications on my part — in consideration of the light which I have it in my power to throw upon many very important branches of physical and metaphysical science — I must solicit, through the influence of your honorable body, a pardon for the crime of which I have been guilty in the death of the creditors upon my departure from Rotterdam. This, then, is the object of the present paper. Its bearer, an inhabitant of the moon, whom I have prevailed upon, and properly instructed, to be my messenger to the earth, will await your Excellencies' pleasure, and return to me with the pardon in question, if it can, in any manner, be obtained.

I have the honor to be, &c., your Excellencies' very humble servant,

HANS PFAALL.

Upon finishing the perusal of this very extraordinary document, Professor Rubadub, it is said, dropped his pipe upon the ground in the extremity of his surprise, and Mynheer Superbus Von Underduk having taken off his spectacles, wiped them, and deposited them in his pocket, so far forgot both himself and his dignity, as to turn round three times upon his heel in the quintessence of astonishment and admiration. There was no doubt about the matter — the pardon should be obtained. So at least swore, with a round oath, Professor Rubadub, and so finally thought the illustrious Von Underduk, as he took the arm of his brother in science, and without saying a word, began to make the best of his way home to deliberate upon the measures to be adopted. Having reached the door, however, of the burgomaster's dwelling, the professor ventured to suggest that as the messenger had thought proper to disappear — no doubt frightened to death by the savage appearance of the burghers of Rotterdam —

the pardon would be of little use, as no one but a man of the moon would undertake a voyage to so vast a distance. To the truth of this observation the burgomaster assented, and the matter was therefore at an end. Not so, however, rumors and speculations. The letter, having been published, gave rise to a variety of gossip and opinion. Some of the over-wise even made themselves ridiculous by decrying the whole business as nothing better than a hoax. But hoax, with these sort of people, is, I believe, a general term for all matters above their comprehension. For my part, I cannot conceive upon what data they have founded such an accusation. Let us see what they say:

Imprimis. That certain wags in Rotterdam have certain especial antipathies to certain burgomasters and astronomers.

Secondly. That an odd little dwarf and bottle conjurer, both of whose ears, for some misdemeanor, have been cut off close to his head, has been missing for several days from the neighboring city of Bruges.

Thirdly. That the newspapers which were stuck all over the little balloon, were newspapers of Holland, and therefore could not have been made in the moon. They were dirty papers — very dirty — and Gluck, the printer, would take his bible oath to their having been printed in Rotterdam.

Fourthly. That Hans Pfaall himself, the drunken villain, and the three very idle gentlemen styled his creditors, were all seen, no longer than two or three days ago, in a tippling house in the suburbs, having just returned, with money in their pockets, from a trip beyond the sea.

Lastly. That it is an opinion very generally received, or which ought to be generally received, that the College of Astronomers in the city of Rotterdam, as well as all other colleges in all other parts of the world, — not to mention colleges and astronomers in general, — are, to say the least of the matter, not a whit better, nor greater, nor wiser than they ought to be.

NOTE. — Strictly speaking, there is but little similarity between the above sketchy trifle, and the celebrated "Moon-Story" of Mr. Locke; but as both have the character of hoaxes, (although the one is in a tone of banter, the other of downright earnest,) and as both hoaxes are on the same subject, the moon — moreover, as both attempt to give plausibility by scientific detail — the author of "Hans Pfaall" thinks it necessary to say, in self-defence, that his own jeu d'esprit was published, in the "Southern Literary Messenger," about three weeks before the commencement of Mr. L's in the "New York Sun." Fancying a likeness which, perhaps, does not exist, some of the New York papers copied "Hans Pfaall," and collated it with the "Moon-Hoax," by way of detecting the writer of the one in the writer of the other.

As many more persons were actually gulled by the "Moon-Hoax" than would be willing to acknowledge the fact, it may here afford some little amusement to show why no one should have been deceived — to point out those particulars of the story which should have been sufficient to establish its real character. Indeed, however rich the imagination displayed in this ingenious fiction, it wanted much of the force which might have been given it by a more scrupulous attention to facts and to general analogy. That the public were misled, even for an instant, merely proves the gross ignorance which is so generally prevalent upon subjects of an astronomical nature.

The moon's distance from the earth is, in round numbers, 240,000 miles. If we desire to ascertain how near, apparently, a lens would bring the satellite, (or any distant object,) we, of course, have but to divide the distance by the magnifying, or more strictly, by the space-penetrating power of the glass. Mr. L. makes his lens have a power of 42,000 times. By this divide 240,000 (the moon's real distance,) and we have five miles and five-sevenths, as the apparent distance. No animal at all could be seen so far; much less the minute points particularized in the story. Mr. L. speaks about Sir John Herschel's perceiving flowers (the Papaver rheas [[rhoeas]], &c.,) and even detecting the color and the shape of the eyes of small birds. Shortly before, too, he has himself observed that the lens would not render perceptible objects of less than eighteen inches in diameter; but even this, as I have said, is giving the glass by far too great power. It may be observed, in passing, that this prodigious glass is said to have been moulded at the glass-house of Messrs. Hartley and Grant, in Dumbarton; but Messrs. H. and G.'s establishment had ceased operations for many years previous to the publication of the hoax.

On page 13, pamphlet edition, speaking of "a hairy veil"

over the eyes of a species of bison, the author says — "It immediately occurred to the acute mind of Dr. Herschel that this was a providential contrivance to protect the eyes of the animal from the great extremes of light and darkness to which all the inhabitants of our side of the moon are periodically subjected." But this cannot be thought a very "acute" observation of the Doctor's. The inhabitants of our side of the moon have, evidently, no darkness at all; so there can be nothing of the "extremes" mentioned. In the absence of the sun they have a light from the earth equal to that of thirteen full unclouded moons.

The topography throughout, even when professing to accord with Blunt's Lunar Chart, is entirely at variance with that or any other lunar chart, and even grossly at variance with itself. The points of the compass, too, are in inextricable confusion; the writer appearing to be ignorant that, on a lunar map, these are not in accordance with terrestrial points; the east being to the left, &c.

Deceived, perhaps, by the vague titles, Mare Nubium, Mare Tranquillitatis, Mare Fæcunditatis, &c., given to the dark spots by former astronomers, Mr. L. has entered into details regarding oceans and other large bodies of water in the moon; whereas there is no astronomical point more positively ascertained than that no such bodies exist there. In examining the boundary between light and darkness (in the crescent or gibbous moon) where this boundary crosses any of the dark places, the line of division is found to be rough and jagged; but, were these dark places liquid, it would evidently be even.

The description of the wings of the man-bat, on page 21, is but a literal copy of Peter Wilkins' account of the wings of his flying islanders. This simple fact should have induced suspicion, at least, it might be thought.

On page 23, we have the following: "What a prodigious influence must our thirteen times larger globe have exercised upon this satellite when an embryo in the womb of time, the passive subject of chemical affinity!" This is very fine; but it should be observed that no astronomer would have made such remark, especially to any Journal of Science; for the earth, in the sense intended, is not only thirteen, but forty-nine times larger than the moon. A similar objection applies to the whole of the concluding pages, where, by way of introduction to some discoveries in Saturn, the philosophical correspondent enters into a minute schoolboy account of that planet: — this to the Edinburgh Journal of Science!

But there is one point, in particular, which should have betrayed the fiction. Let us imagine the power actually possessed of seeing animals upon the moon's surface; — what would first arrest the attention of an observer from the earth? Certainly neither their shape, size, nor any other such peculiarity, so soon as their remarkable situation. They would appear to be walking, with heels up and head down, in the manner of flies on a ceiling. The real observer would have uttered an instant ejaculation of surprise (however prepared by previous knowledge) at the singularity of their position; the fictitious observer has not even mentioned the subject, but speaks of seeing the entire bodies of such creatures, when it is demonstrable that he could have seen only the diameter of their heads!

It might as well be remarked, in conclusion, that the size, and particularly the powers of the man-bats (for example, their ability to fly in so rare an atmosphere — if, indeed, the moon have any) — with most of the other fancies in regard to animal and vegetable existence, are at variance, generally, with all analogical reasoning on these themes; and that analogy here will often amount to conclusive demonstration. It is, perhaps, scarcely necessary to add, that all the suggestions attributed to Brewster and Herschel, in the beginning of the article, about "a transfusion of artificial light through the focal object of vision," &c., &c., belong to that species of figurative writing which come [[comes]], most properly, under the denomination of rigmarole.

There is a real and very definite limit to optical discovery among the stars — a limit whose nature need only be stated to be understood. If, indeed, the casting of large lenses were all that is required, man's ingenuity would ultimately prove equal to the task, and we might have them of any size demanded. But, unhappily, in proportion to the increase of size in the lens, and, consequently, of space-penetrating power, is the diminution of light from the object, by diffusion of its rays. And for this evil there is no remedy within human ability; for an object is seen by means of that light alone which proceeds from itself, whether direct or reflected. Thus the only "artificial" light which could avail Mr. Locke, would be some artificial light which he should be able to throw — not upon the "focal object of vision," but upon the real object to be viewed — to wit: upon the moon. It has been easily calculated that, when the light proceeding from a star becomes so diffused as to be as weak as the natural light proceeding from the whole of the stars, in a clear and moonless night, then the star is no longer visible for any practical purpose.

The Earl of Ross telescope, lately constructed in England, has a speculum with a reflecting surface of 4071 square inches; the Herschel telescope having one of only 1811. The metal of the Earl of Ross' is 6 feet diameter; it is 5 1/2 inches thick at the edges, and 5 at the centre. The weight is 3 tons. The focal length is 50 feet.

I have lately read a singular and somewhat ingenious little book, whose title page runs thus: — "L'Homme dans la lvne, ou le Voyage Chimerique fait au Monde de la Lvne, nouuellement decouuert par Dominique Gonzales, Aduanturier Espagnol, autremèt dit le Courier volant. Mis en notre langve par J. B. D. A. Paris, chez Francois Piot, pres la Fontaine de Saint Benoist. Et chez J. Goignard, au premier pilier de la grand' salle du Palais, proche les Consultations, MDCXLVIII." pp. 176.

The writer professes to have translated his work from the English of one Mr. D'Avisson (Davidson?) although there is a terrible ambiguity in the statement. "J'en ai eu," says he, "l'original de Monsieur D'Avisson, medecin des mieux versez qui soient aujourd'huy dans la cònoissance des Belles

Lettres, et sur tout de la Philosophie Naturelle. Je lui ai cette obligation entre les autres, de m'auoir non seulement mis en main ce Livre en anglois, mais encore le Manuscrit du Sieur Thomas D'Anan, gentilhomme Eccossois, recommandable pour sa vertu, sur la version duquel j'advoue que j'ay tiré le plan de la mienne."

After some irrelevant adventures, much in the manner of Gil Blas, and which occupy the first thirty pages, the author relates that, being ill during a sea voyage, the crew abandoned him, together with a negro servant, on the island of St. Helena. To increase the chances of obtaining food, the two separate, and live as far apart as possible. This brings about a training of birds, to serve the purpose of carrier-pigeons between them. By and by these are taught to carry parcels of some weight — and this weight is gradually increased. At length the idea is entertained of uniting the force of a great number of the birds, with a view to raising the author himself. A machine is contrived for the purpose, and we have a minute description of it, which is materially helped out by a steel engraving. Here we perceive the Signor Gonzales, with point ruffles and a huge periwig, seated astride something which resembles very closely a broomstick, and borne aloft by a multitude of wild swans (ganzas) who had strings reaching from their tails to the machine.

The main event detailed in the Signor's narrative depends upon a very important fact, of which the reader is kept in ignorance until near the end of the book. The ganzas, with whom he had become so familiar, were not really denizens of

St. Helena, but of the moon. Thence it had been their custom, time out of mind, to migrate annually to some portion of the earth. In proper season, of course they would return home; and the author, happening, one day, to require their services for a short voyage, is unexpectedly carried straight up, and in a very brief period arrives at the satellite. Here he finds, among other odd things, that the people enjoy extreme happiness; that they have no law; that they die without pain; that they are from ten to thirty feet in height; that they live five thousand years; that they have an emperor called Irdonozur; and that they can jump sixty feet high, when, being out of the gravitating influence, they fly about with fans.

I cannot forbear giving a specimen of the general philosophy of the volume.

"I must now declare to you," says the Signor Gonzales, "the nature of the place in which I found myself. All the clouds were beneath my feet, or, if you please, spread between me and the earth. As to the stars, since there was no night where I was, they always had the same appearance; not brilliant, as usual, but pale, and very nearly like the moon of a morning. But few of them were visible, and these ten times larger (as well as I could judge,) than they seem to the inhabitants of the earth. The moon which wanted two days of being full, was of a terrible bigness.

"I must not forget here, that the stars appeared only on that side of the globe turned towards the moon, and that the closer they were to it the larger they seemed. I have also to inform you that, whether it was calm weather or stormy,

I found myself always immediately between the moon and the earth. I was convinced of this for two reasons — because my birds always flew in a straight line; and because whenever we attempted to rest, we were carried insensibly around the globe of the earth. For I admit the opinion of Copernicus, who maintains that it never ceases to revolve from the east to the west, not upon the poles of the Equinoctial, commonly called the poles of the world, but upon those of the Zodiac, a question of which I propose to speak more at length hereafter, when I shall have leisure to refresh my memory in regard to the astrology which I learned at Salamanca when young, and have since forgotten."

Notwithstanding the blunders italicised, the book is not without some claim to attention, as affording a näive specimen of the current astronomical notions of the time. One of these assumed, that the "gravitating power" extended but a short distance from the earth's surface, and, accordingly, we find our voyager "carried insensibly around the globe," &c.

There have been other "voyages to the moon," but none of higher merit than the one just mentioned. That of Bergerac is utterly meaningless. In the third volume of the "American Quarterly Review" will be found quite an elaborate criticism upon a certain "Journey" of the kind in question; — a criticism in which it is difficult to say whether the critic most exposes the stupidity of the book, or his own absurd ignorance of astronomy. I forget the title of the work; but the means of the voyage are more deplorably ill conceived than are even the ganzas of our friend the Signor Gonzales. The adventurer, in digging the earth, happens to discover a peculiar metal for which the moon has a strong attraction, and straightway constructs of it a box, which, when cast loose from its terrestrial fastenings, flies with him, forthwith, to the satellite. The "Flight of Thomas O'Rourke," is a jeu d'esprit not altogether contemptible, and has been translated into German. Thomas, the hero, was, in fact, the game-keeper of an Irish peer, whose eccentricities gave rise to the tale. The "flight" is made on an eagle's back, from Hungry Hill, a lofty mountain at the end of Bantry Bay.

In these various brochures the aim is always satirical; the theme being a description of Lunarian customs as compared with ours. In none, is there any effort at plausibility in the details of the voyage itself. The writers seem, in each instance, to be utterly uninformed in respect to astronomy. In "Hans Pfaall" the design is original, inasmuch as regards an attempt at verisimilitude, in the application of scientific principles (so far as the whimsical nature of the subject would permit,) to the actual passage between the earth and the moon.

The Conversation of Eiros and Charmion

EIROS. Why do you call me Eiros?

CHARMION. So henceforward will you always be called. You must forget, too, my earthly name, and speak to me as Charmion.

EIROS. This is indeed no dream!

CHARMION. Dreams are with us no more — but of these mysteries anon. I rejoice to see you looking life-like and rational. The film of the shadow has already passed from off your eyes. Be of heart, and fear nothing. Your allotted days of stupor have expired; and, to-morrow, I will myself induct you into the full joys and wonders of your novel existence.

EIROS. True — I feel no stupor — none at all. The wild sickness and the terrible darkness have left me, and I hear no longer that mad, rushing, horrible sound, like the "voice of many waters." Yet my senses are bewildered, Charmion, with the keenness of their perception of the new.

CHARMION. A few days will remove all this — but I fully understand you, and feel for you. It is now ten earthly years since I underwent what you undergo — yet the remembrance of it hangs by me still. You have now suffered all of pain, however, which you will suffer in Aidenn.

EIROS. In Aidenn?

CHARMION. In Aidenn.

EIROS. Oh God! — pity me, Charmion! — I am overburthened with the majesty of all things — of the unknown now known — of the speculative Future merged in the august and certain Present.

CHARMION. Grapple not now with such thoughts. To-morrow we will speak of this. Your mind wavers, and its agitation will find relief in the exercise of simple memories. Look not around, nor forward — but back. I am burning with anxiety to hear the details of that stupendous event which threw you among us. Tell me of it. Let us converse of familiar things, in the old familiar language of the world which has so fearfully perished.

EIROS. Most fearfully, fearfully! — this is indeed no dream.

CHARMION. Dreams are no more. Was I much mourned, my Eiros?

EIROS. Mourned, Charmion? — oh deeply. To that last hour of all there hung a cloud of intense gloom and devout sorrow over your household.

CHARMION. And that last hour — speak of it. Remember that, beyond the naked fact of the catastrophe itself, I know nothing. When, coming out from among mankind, I passed into Night through the Grave — at that period, if I remember aright, the calamity which overwhelmed you was utterly unanticipated. But, indeed, I knew little of the speculative philosophy of the day.

EIROS. The individual calamity was, as you say, entirely unanticipated; but analogous misfortunes had been long a subject of discussion with astronomers. I need scarce tell you, my friend, that, even when you left us, men had agreed to understand those passages in the most holy writings which speak of the final destruction of all things by fire, as having reference to the orb of the earth alone. But in regard to the immediate agency of the ruin, speculation had been at fault from that epoch in astronomical knowledge in which the comets were divested of the terrors of flame. The very moderate density of these bodies had been well established. They had been observed to pass among the satellites of Jupiter, without bringing about any sensible alteration either in the masses or in the orbits of these secondary planets. We had long regarded the wanderers as vapory creations of inconceivable tenuity, and as altogether incapable of doing injury to our substantial globe, even in the event of contact. But contact was not in any degree dreaded; for the elements of all the comets were accurately known. That among them we should look for the agency of the threatened fiery destruction had been for many years considered an inadmissible idea. But wonders and wild fancies had been, of late days, strangely rife among mankind; and, although it was only with a few of the ignorant that actual apprehension prevailed, upon the announcement by astronomers of a new comet, yet this announcement was generally received with I know not what of agitation and mistrust.

The elements of the strange orb were immediately calculated, and it was at once conceded by all observers that its path, at perihelion, would bring it into very close proximity with the earth. There were two or three astronomers, and these of secondary note, who resolutely maintained that a contact was inevitable. I cannot very well express to you the effect of this intelligence upon the people. For a few short days they would not believe an assertion which their intellect, so long employed among worldly considerations, could not in any manner grasp. But the truth of a vitally important fact soon makes its way into the understanding of even the most stolid. Finally, all men saw that astronomical knowledge lied not, and they awaited the comet. Its approach was not, at first, seemingly rapid — nor was its appearance of very unusual character. It was of a dull red, and had little perceptible train. For seven or eight days we saw no material increase in its apparent diameter, and but a partial alteration in its color. Meantime, the ordinary affairs of men were discarded, and all interests absorbed in a growing discussion, instituted by the philosophic, in respect to the cometary nature. Even the grossly ignorant aroused their sluggish capacities to such considerations. The learned now gave their intellect — their soul — to no such points as the allaying of fear, or to the sustenance of loved theory. They sought — they panted for right views. They groaned for perfected knowledge. Truth arose in the purity of her strength and exceeding majesty, and the wise bowed down and adored.

That material injury to our globe or to its inhabitants would result from the apprehended contact, was an opinion which hourly lost ground among the wise — and the wise were now freely permitted to rule the reason and the fancy of the crowd. It was demonstrated, that the density of the comet's nucleus was far less than that of our rarest gas; and the harmless passage among the satellites of Jupiter was a point strongly insisted upon, and which served greatly to allay terror. Theologists, with an earnestness fear-enkindled, dwelt upon the biblical prophecies, and expounded them to the people with a directness and simplicity, of which no previous instance had been known. That the final destruction of the earth must be brought about by the agency of fire, was urged with a spirit that enforced every where conviction; and that the comets were of no fiery nature (as all men now knew) was a truth which relieved all, in a great measure, from the apprehension of the great calamity foretold. It is noticeable that the popular prejudices and vulgar errors in regard to pestilences and wars — errors which were wont to prevail upon every appearance of a comet — were now altogether unknown. As if by some sudden convulsive exertion, reason had at once hurled superstition from her throne. The feeblest understanding had derived vigor from excessive interest.

What minor evils might arise from the contact were points of elaborate question. The learned spoke of slight geological disturbances; of probable alterations in climate, and consequently in vegetation; of possible magnetic and electric influences. Many held that no visible or perceptible effect would in any manner be produced. While such discussions were going on, their subject gradually approached, growing larger in apparent diameter, and of a more brilliant lustre. Mankind grew paler as it came. All human operations were suspended.

There was an epoch in the course of the general sentiment

when the comet had attained at length a size surpassing that of any previously recorded visitation. The people, now, dismissing any lingering hope that the astronomers were wrong, experienced all the certainty of evil. The chimerical aspect of their terror was gone. The hearts of the stoutest of our race beat violently within their bosoms. A very few days sufficed, however, to merge even such feelings in sentiments more unendurable. We could no longer apply to the strange orb any accustomed thoughts. Its historical attributes had disappeared. It oppressed us with a hideous novelty of emotion. We saw it not as an astronomical phenomenon in the heavens — but as an incubus upon our heart, and a shadow upon our brain. It had taken, with inconceivable rapidity, the character of a gigantic mantle of rare flame extending from horizon to horizon.

Yet a day, and men breathed with greater freedom. It was clear that we were already within the influence of the comet — yet we lived. We even felt an unusual elasticity of frame and vivacity of mind. The exceeding tenuity of the object of our dread was apparent; all heavenly objects were plainly visible through it. Meantime, our vegetation had perceptibly altered — and we gained faith, from this predicted circumstance, in the foresight of the wise. A wild luxuriance of foliage — utterly unknown before — burst out upon every vegetable thing.

Yet another day — and the evil was not altogether upon us. It was now evident that its nucleus would first reach us. A wild change had come over all men — and the first sense of pain was the wild signal for general lamentation and horror. This first sense of pain lay in a rigorous constriction of the breast and lungs, and an insufferable dryness of the skin. It could not be denied that our atmosphere was radically affected — the conformation of this atmosphere and the possible modifications to which it might be subjected, were now the topics of discussion. The result of investigation sent an electric thrill of the intensest terror through the universal heart of man.

It had been long known that the air which encircled us was a compound of oxygen and nitrogen gases, in the proportion of twenty-one measures of oxygen, and seventy-nine of nitrogen, in every one hundred of the atmosphere. Oxygen, which was the principle of combustion, and the vehicle of heat, was absolutely necessary to the support of animal life, and was the most powerful and energetic agent in nature. Nitrogen, on the contrary, was incapable of supporting either animal life or flame. An unnatural excess of oxygen would result, it had been ascertained, in just such an elevation of the animal spirits as we had latterly experienced. It was the pursuit, the extension of the idea, which had engendered awe. What would be the result of a total extraction of the nitrogen? A combustion irresistible, all-devouring, omni-prevalent, immediate — the entire fulfilment, in all its minute and terrible details, of the fiery and horror-inspiring denunciations of the prophecies of the Holy Book.

Why need I paint, Charmion, the now disenchained frenzy of mankind? That tenuity in the comet which had previously inspired us with hope, was now the source of the bitterness of despair. In its impalpable gaseous character we clearly perceived the consummation of Fate. Meantime a day again passed — bearing away with it the last shadow of Hope. We gasped in the rapid modification of the air. The red blood bounded tumultuously through its strict channels. A furious delirium possessed all men; and, with arms immoveably outstretched towards the threatening Heavens, they trembled and shrieked aloud. But the nucleus of the destroyer was now upon us. Even here in Aidenn, I shudder while I speak. Let me be brief — brief as the ruin that overwhelmed. For a short moment there was a wild lurid light alone, visiting and penetrating all things. Then — let us bow down, Charmion, before the excessive majesty of the great God! — then, there came a great pervading sound, as if from the mouth itself of HIM; while the whole incumbent mass of ether in which we existed burst at once into a species of intense flame, for whose surpassing brilliancy and all-fervid heat even the angels in the high Heaven of pure knowledge have no name. Thus ended all.

A Descent into the Maelström

WE had now reached the summit of the loftiest crag. For some minutes the old man seemed too much exhausted to speak.

"Not long ago," said he, at length, "and I could have guided you on this route as well as the youngest of my sons; but, about three years past, there happened to me an event such as never happened before to mortal man — or at least such as no man ever survived to tell of — and the six hours of deadly terror which I then endured have broken me up body and soul. You suppose me a very old man — but I am not. It took less than a single day to change these hairs from a jetty black to white, to weaken my limbs, and to unstring my nerves, so that I tremble at the least exertion, and am frightened at a shadow. Do you know I can scarcely look over this little cliff without getting giddy?"

The "little cliff," upon whose edge he had so carelessly thrown himself down to rest, that the weightier portion of his body hung over it, while he was only kept from falling by the tenure of his elbow on its extreme and slippery edge — this "little cliff" arose, a sheer unobstructed precipice of black shining rock, some fifteen or sixteen hundred feet from the world of crags beneath us. No consideration would have tempted me to within half a dozen yards of its brink. In truth so deeply was I excited by the perilous position of my companion, that I fell at full length upon the ground, clung to the shrubs around me, and dared not even glance upward at the sky — while I struggled in vain to divest myself of the idea that the very foundations of the mountain were in danger from the fury of the winds. It was long before I could reason myself into sufficient courage to sit up and look out into the distance.

"You must get over these fancies," said the guide, "for I have brought you here that you might have the best possible view of the scene of that event I mentioned — and to tell you the whole story with the spot just under your eye."

"We are now," he continued, in that particularising manner which distinguished him — "we are now close upon the Norwegian coast — in the sixty-eighth degree of latitude — in the great province of Nordland — and in the dreary district of Lofoden. The mountain upon whose top we sit is Helseggen, the Cloudy. Now raise yourself up a little higher — hold on to the grass if you feel giddy — so — and look out beyond the belt of vapor beneath us into the sea."

I looked dizzily, and beheld a wide expanse of ocean, whose waters wore so inky a hue as to bring at once to my mind the Nubian Geographer's account of the Mare Tenebrarum. A panorama more deplorably desolate no human imagination can conceive. To the right and left, as far as the eye could reach, there lay outstretched, like ramparts of the world, lines of horridly black and beetling cliff, whose character of irredeemable gloom was but the more forcibly illustrated by the surf which reared high up against it its white and ghastly crest, howling and shrieking forever. Just opposite the promontory upon whose apex we were placed, and at a distance of some five or six miles out at sea, there was visible a small, bleak-looking island; or, more properly, its position was discernible through the wilderness of surge in which it was enveloped. About two miles nearer the land, arose another of smaller size, hideously craggy and barren, and encompassed at various intervals by a cluster of dark rocks.

The appearance of the ocean, in the space between the more distant island and the shore, had something very unusual about it. Although, at the time, so strong a gale was blowing landward that a brig in the remote offing lay to under a double-reefed trysail, and constantly plunged her whole hull out of sight, still there was here nothing like a regular swell, but only a short, quick, angry cross-dashing of water in every direction — as well in the teeth of the wind as otherwise. Of foam there was little, except in the immediate vicinity of the rocks.

"The island in the distance," resumed the old man, "is called by the Norwegians Vurrgh. The one midway is Moskoe. That a mile to the northward is Ambaaren. Yonder are Islesen, Hotholm, Keildhelm, Suarven, and Buckholm. Farther off — between Moskoe and Vurrgh — are Otterholm, Flimen, Sandflesen, and Stockholm. These are the true names of the places — but why it has been thought necessary to name them at all, is more than either you or I can understand. Do you hear any thing? Do you see any change in the water?"

We had now been about ten minutes upon the top of Helseggen, to which we had ascended from the interior of Lofoden, so that we had caught no glimpse of the sea until it had burst upon us from the summit. As the old man spoke I became aware of a loud and gradually increasing sound, like the moaning of a vast herd of buffaloes upon an American prairie; and at the same moment I perceived that what seamen term the chopping character of the ocean beneath us was rapidly changing into a current which set to the eastward. Even while I gazed, this current acquired a monstrous velocity. Each moment added to its speed — to its headlong impetuosity. In five minutes the whole sea, as far as Vurrgh, was lashed into ungovernable fury; but it was between Moskoe and the coast that the main uproar held its sway. Here the vast bed of the waters, seamed and scarred into a thousand conflicting channels, burst suddenly into phrensied convulsion — heaving, boiling, hissing — gyrating in gigantic and innumerable vortices, and all whirling and plunging on to the eastward with a rapidity which water never elsewhere assumes except in precipitous descents.

In a few minutes more, there came over the scene another radical alteration. The general surface grew somewhat more smooth, and the whirlpools, one by one, disappeared, while prodigious streaks of foam became apparent where none had been seen before. These streaks, at length, spreading out to a great distance, and entering into combination, took unto themselves the gyratory motion of the subsided vortices, and seemed to form the germ of another more vast. Suddenly — very suddenly — this assumed a distinct and definite existence, in a circle of more than a mile in diameter. The edge of the whirl was represented by a broad belt of gleaming spray — but no particle of this slipped into the mouth of the terrific funnel, whose interior, as far as the eye could fathom it, was a smooth, shining, and jet-black wall of water, inclined to the horizon at an angle of some forty-five degrees, speeding dizzily round and round with a swaying and sweltering motion, and sending forth to the winds an appalling voice, half shriek, half roar, such as not even the mighty cataract of Niagara ever lifts up in its agony to Heaven.

The mountain trembled to its very base, and the rock rocked. I threw myself upon my face, and clung to the scant herbage in an excess of nervous agitation.

"This," said I at length, to the old man — "this can be nothing else than the great whirlpool of the Maelström."

"So it is sometimes termed," said he. "We Norwegians call it the Moskoe-ström, from the island of Moskoe in the midway."

The ordinary accounts of this vortex had by no means prepared me for what I saw. That of Jonas Ramus, which is perhaps the most circumstantial of any, cannot impart the faintest conception either of the magnificence, or of the horror of the scene — or of the wild bewildering sense of the novel which confounds the beholder. I am not sure from what point of view the writer in question surveyed it, nor at what time — but it could neither have been from the summit of Helseggen, nor during a storm. There are some passages of his description, nevertheless, which may be quoted for their details, although their effect is exceedingly feeble in conveying an impression of the spectacle.

"Between Lofoden and Moskoe," he says, "the depth of the water is between thirty-six and forty fathoms; but on the other side, toward Ver (Vurrgh) this depth decreases so as not to afford a convenient passage for a vessel, without the risk of splitting on the rocks, which happens even in the calmest weather. When it is flood, the stream runs up the country between Lofoden and Moskoe with a boisterous rapidity; but the roar of its impetuous ebb to the sea is scarce equalled by the loudest and most dreadful cataracts; the noise being heard several leagues off, and the vortices or pits are of such an extent and depth, that if a ship comes within its attraction, it is inevitably absorbed and carried down to the bottom, and there beat to pieces against the rocks; and when the water relaxes the fragments thereof are thrown up again. But these intervals of tranquility are only at the turn of the ebb and flood, and in calm weather, and last but a quarter of an hour, its violence gradually returning. When the stream is most boisterous, and its fury heightened by a storm, it is dangerous to come within a Norway mile of it. Boats, yachts, and ships have been carried away by not guarding against it before they were within its reach. It likewise happens frequently, that whales come too near the stream, and are overpowered by its violence; and then it is impossible to describe their howlings and bellowings in their fruitless struggles to disengage themselves. A bear once, attempting to swim from Lofoden to Moskoe, was caught by the stream and borne down, while he roared terribly, so as to be heard on shore.

Large stocks of firs and pine trees, after being absorbed by the current, rise again broken and torn to such a degree as if bristles grew upon them. This plainly shows the bottom to consist of craggy rocks, among which they are whirled to and fro. This stream is regulated by the flux and reflux of the sea — it being constantly high and low water every six hours. In the year 1645, early in the morning of Sexagesima Sunday, it raged with such noise and impetuosity that the very stones of the houses on the coast fell to the ground."

In regard to the depth of the water, I could not see how this could have been ascertained at all in the immediate vicinity of the vortex. The "forty fathoms" must have reference only to portions of the channel close upon the shore either of Moskoe or Lofoden. The depth in the centre of the Moskoe-ström must be immeasurably greater; and no better proof of this fact is necessary than can be obtained from even the sidelong glance into the abyss of the whirl which may be had from the highest crag of Helseggen. Looking down from this pinnacle upon the howling Phlegethon below, I could not help smiling at the simplicity with which the honest Jonas Ramus records, as a matter difficult of belief, the anecdotes of the whales and the bears; for it appeared to me, in fact, a self-evident thing that the largest ship of the line in existence, coming within the influence of that deadly attraction, could resist it as little as a feather the hurricane, and must disappear bodily and at once.

The attempts to account for the phenomenon — some of which, I remember, seemed to me sufficiently plausible in perusal — now wore a very different and unsatisfactory aspect. The idea generally received is that this, as well as three smaller vortices among the Ferroe islands, "have no other cause than the collision of waves rising and falling, at flux and reflux, against a ridge of rocks and shelves, which confines the water so that it precipitates itself like a cataract; and thus the higher the flood rises, the deeper must the fall be, and the natural result of all is a whirlpool or vortex, the prodigious suction of which is sufficiently known by lesser experiments." — These are the words of the Encyclopædia Britannica. Kircher and others imagine that in the centre of the channel of the Maelström is an abyss penetrating the globe, and issuing in some very remote part — the Gulf of Bothnia being somewhat decidedly named in one instance. This opinion, idle in itself, was the one to which, as I gazed, my imagination most readily assented; and, mentioning it to the guide, I was rather surprised to hear him say that, although it was the view almost universally entertained of the subject by the Norwegians, it nevertheless was not his own. As to the former notion he confessed his inability to comprehend it; and here I agreed with him — for, however conclusive on paper, it becomes altogether unintelligible, and even absurd, amid the thunder of the abyss.

"You have had a good look at the whirl now," said the old man, "and if you will creep round this crag, so as to get in its lee, and deaden the roar of the water, I will tell you a story that will convince you I ought to know something of the Moskoe-ström."

I placed myself as desired, and he proceeded.

"Myself and my two brothers once owned a schooner-rigged smack of about seventy tons burthen, with which we were in the habit of fishing among the islands beyond Moskoe, nearly to Vurrgh. In all violent eddies at sea there is good fishing, at proper opportunities, if one has only the courage to attempt it; but among the whole of the Lofoden coastmen, we three were the only ones who made a regular business of going out to the islands, as I tell you. The usual grounds are a great way lower down to the southward. There fish can be got at all hours, without much risk, and therefore these places are preferred. The choice spots over here among the rocks, however, not only yield the finest variety, but in far greater abundance; so that we often got in a single day what the more timid of the craft could not scrape together in a week. In fact, we made it a matter of desperate speculation — the risk of life standing instead of labor, and courage answering for capital.

"We kept the smack in a cove about five miles higher up the coast than this; and it was our practice, in fine weather, to take advantage of the fifteen minutes' slack to push across the main channel of the Moskoe-ström, far above the pool, and then drop down upon anchorage somewhere near Otterholm, or Sandflesen, where the eddies are not so violent as elsewhere. Here we used to remain until nearly time for slack-water again, when we weighed and made for home. We never set out upon this expedition without a steady side wind for going and coming — one that we felt sure would not fail us before our return — and we seldom made a mis-calculation upon this point. Twice, during six years, we were forced to stay all night at anchor on account of a dead calm, which is a rare thing indeed just about here; and once we had to remain on the grounds nearly a week, starving to death, owing to a gale which blew up shortly after our arrival, and made the channel too boisterous to be thought of. Upon this occasion we should have been driven out to sea in spite of every thing, (for the whirlpools threw us round and round so violently, that at length we fouled our anchor and dragged it) if it had not been that we drifted into one of the innumerable cross currents — here to-day and gone to-morrow — which drove us under the lee of Flimen, where, by good luck, we brought up.

"I could not tell you the twentieth part of the difficulties we encountered 'on the grounds' — it is a bad spot to be in even in good weather — but we made shift always to run the gauntlet of the Moskoe-ström itself without accident; although at times my heart has been in my mouth when we happened to be a minute or so behind or before the slack. The wind sometimes was not as strong as we thought it at starting, and then we made rather less way than we could wish, while the current rendered the smack unmanageable. My eldest brother had a son eighteen years old, and I had two stout boys of my own. These would have been of great assistance at such times, in using the sweeps, as well as afterward in fishing — but, somehow, although we ran the risk ourselves, we had not the heart to let the young ones get into the danger — for, after all is said and done, it was a horrible danger, and that is the truth.

"It is now within a few days of three years since what I am going to tell you occurred. It was on the tenth day of July, 18 — , a day which the people of this part of the world will never forget — for it was one in which blew the most terrible hurricane that ever came out of the heavens. And yet all the morning, and indeed until late in the afternoon, there was a gentle and steady breeze from the south-west, while the sun shone brightly, so that the oldest seaman among us could not have foreseen what was to follow.

"The three of us — my two brothers and myself — had crossed over to the islands about two o'clock P. M. and had soon nearly loaded the smack with fine fish, which, we all remarked, were more plenty that day than we had ever known them. It was just seven, by my watch, when we weighed and started for home, so as to make the worst of the Ström at slack water, which we knew would be at eight.

"We set out with a fresh wind on our starboard quarter, and for some time spanked along at a great rate, never dreaming of danger, for indeed we saw not the slightest reason to apprehend it. All at once we were taken aback by a breeze from over Helseggen. This was most unusual — something that had never happened to us before, and I began to feel a little uneasy without exactly knowing why. We put the boat on the wind, but could make no headway at all for the eddies, and I was upon the point of proposing to return to the anchorage, when, looking astern, we saw the whole horizon covered with a singular copper-colored cloud that rose with the most amazing velocity.

"In the meantime the breeze that had headed us off fell away, and we were dead becalmed, drifting about in every direction. This state of things, however, did not last long enough to give us time to think about it. In less than a minute the storm was upon us — in less than two the sky was entirely overcast — and what with this and the driving spray, it became suddenly so dark that we could not see each other in the smack.

"Such a hurricane as then blew it is folly to attempt describing. The oldest seaman in Norway never experienced any thing like it. We had let our sails go by the run before it cleverly took us; but at the first puff both our masts went by the board as if they had been sawed off — the mainmast taking with it my youngest brother, who had lashed himself to it for safety.

"Our boat was the lightest feather of a thing that ever sat upon water. It had a complete flush deck with only a small hatch near the bow, and this hatch it had always been our custom to batten down when about to cross the Ström, by way of precaution against the chopping seas. But for this circumstance we should have foundered at once — for we lay entirely buried for some moments. How my elder brother escaped destruction I cannot say, for I never had an opportunity of ascertaining. For my part, as soon as I had let the foresail run, I threw myself flat on deck, with my feet against the narrow gunwale of the bow, and with my hands grasping a ring-bolt near the foot of the foremast. It was mere instinct that prompted me to do this — which was undoubtedly the very best thing I could have done — for I was too much flurried to think.

"For some moments we were completely deluged, as I say, and all this time I held my breath, and clung to the bolt. When I could stand it no longer I raised myself upon my knees, still keeping hold with my hands, and thus got my head clear. Presently our little boat gave herself a shake, just as a dog does in coming out of the water, and thus rid herself, in some measure, of the seas. I was now trying to get the better of the stupor that had come over me, and to collect my senses so as to see what was to be done, when I felt somebody grasp my arm. It was my elder brother, and my heart leaped for joy, for I had made sure that he was overboard — but the next moment all this joy was turned into horror — for he put his mouth close to my ear, and screamed out the word 'Moskoe-ström!'

"No one ever will know what my feelings were at that moment. I shook from head to foot as if I had had the most violent fit of the ague. I knew what he meant by that one word well enough — I knew what he wished to make me understand. With the wind that now drove us on, we were bound for the whirl of the Ström, and nothing could save us!

"You perceive that in crossing the Ström channel, we always went a long way up above the whirl, even in the calmest weather, and then had to wait and watch carefully for the slack — but now we were driving right upon the pool itself, and in such a hurricane as this! 'To be sure,' I thought, 'we shall get there just about the slack — there is some little hope in that' — but in the next moment I cursed myself for being so great a fool as to dream of hope at all. I knew very well that we were doomed, had we been ten times a ninety-gun ship.

"By this time the first fury of the tempest had spent itself, or perhaps we did not feel it so much, as we scudded before it, but at all events the seas, which at first had been kept down by the wind, and lay flat and frothing, now got up into absolute mountains. A singular change, too, had come over the heavens. Around in every direction it was still as black as pitch, but nearly overhead there burst out, all at once, a circular rift of clear sky — as clear as I ever saw — and of a deep bright blue — and through it there blazed forth the full moon with a lustre that I never before knew her to wear. She lit up every thing about us with the greatest distinctness — but, oh God, what a scene it was to light up!

"I now made one or two attempts to speak to my brother — but, in some manner which I could not understand, the din had so increased that I could not make him hear a single word, although I screamed at the top of my voice in his ear. Presently he shook his head, looking as pale as death, and held up one of his finger as if to say 'listen! '

"At first I could not make out what he meant — but soon a hideous thought flashed upon me. I dragged my watch from its fob — it was not going. I glanced at its face by the moonlight, and then burst into tears as I flung it far away into the ocean. It had run down at seven o'clock! We were behind the time of the slack, and the whirl of the Ström was in full fury!

"When a boat is well built, properly trimmed, and not deep laden, the waves in a strong gale, when she is going large, seem always to slip from beneath her — which appears very strange to a landsman — and this is what is called riding, in sea phrase. Well, so far we had ridden the swells very cleverly; but presently a gigantic sea happened to take us right under the counter, and bore us with it as it rose — up — up — as if into the sky. I would not have believed that any wave could rise so high. And then down we came with a sweep, a slide, and a plunge, that made me feel sick and dizzy, as if I was falling from some lofty mountain-top in a dream. But while we were up I had thrown a quick glance around — and that one glance was all sufficient. I saw our exact position in an instant. The Moskoe-ström whirlpool was about a quarter of a mile dead ahead — but no more like the every-day Moskoe-ström, than a mill-race is like the whirl as you now see it. If I had not known where we were, and what we had to expect, I should not have recognised the place at all. As it was, I involuntarily closed my eyes in horror. The lids clenched themselves together as if in a spasm.

"It could not have been more than two minutes afterward until we suddenly felt the waves subside, and were enveloped in a wilderness of foam. The [page 239:] boat made a sharp half turn to larboard, and then shot off in its new direction like a thunderbolt. At the same moment the roaring noise of the water was completely drowned in a kind of shrill shriek — such a sound as you might imagine given out by the waste-pipes of many thousand steam-vessels, letting off their steam all together. We were now in the belt of surf that always surrounds the whirl, and I thought of course that another moment would plunge us into the abyss — down which we could only see indistinctly on account of the amazing velocity with which we were borne along. The boat did not seem to sink into the water at all, but to skim like an air-bubble upon the surface of the surge. Her starboard side was next the whirl, and on the larboard arose the world of ocean we had left. It stood like a huge writhing wall between us and the horizon.

"It may appear strange, but now, when we were in the very jaws of the gulf, I felt more composed than when we were only approaching it. Having made up my mind to hope no more, I got rid of a great deal of that terror which unmanned me at first. I suppose it was despair that strung my nerves.

"It may look like boasting — but what I tell you is truth — I began to reflect how magnificent a thing it was to die in such a manner, and how foolish it was in me to think of so paltry a consideration as my own individual life, in view of so wonderful a manifestation of God's power. I do believe that I blushed with shame when this idea crossed my mind. After a little while I became possessed with the keenest curiosity about the whirl itself. I positively felt a wish to explore its depths, even at the sacrifice I was going to make; and my principal grief was that I should never be able to tell my old companions on shore about the mysteries I should see. These, no doubt, were singular fancies to occupy a man's mind in such extremity — and I have often thought since, that the revolutions of the boat around the pool might have rendered me a little light-headed.

"There was another circumstance which tended to restore my self-possession; and this was the cessation of the wind, which could not reach us in our present situation — for, as you saw yourself, the belt of surf is considerably lower than the general bed of the ocean, and this latter now towered above us, a high, black, mountainous ridge. If you have never been at sea in a heavy gale, you can form no idea of the confusion of mind occasioned by the wind and spray together. They blind, deafen, and strangle you, and take away all power of action or reflection. But we were now, in a great measure, rid of these annoyances — just us death-condemned felons in prison are allowed petty indulgences, forbidden them while their doom is yet uncertain.

"How often we made the circuit of the belt it is impossible to say. We careered round and round for perhaps an hour, flying rather than floating, getting gradually more and more into the middle of the surge, and then nearer and nearer to its horrible inner edge. All this time I had never let go of the ring-bolt. My brother was at the stern, holding on to a small empty water-cask which had been securely lashed aft under the coop of the counter, and was the only thing on deck that had not been swept overboard when the gale first took us. As we approached the brink of the pit he let go his hold upon this, and made for the ring, from which, in the agony of his terror, he endeavored to force my hands, as it was not large enough to afford us both a secure grasp. I never felt deeper grief than when I saw him attempt this act — although I knew he was a madman when he did it — a raving maniac through sheer fright. I did not care, however, to contest the point with him. I knew it could make no difference whether either of us held on at all; so I let him have the bolt, and went, myself, astern to the cask. This there was no great difficulty in doing; for the smack flew round steadily enough, and upon an even keel — only swaying to and fro, with the immense sweeps and swelters of the whirl. Scarcely had I secured myself in my new position, when we gave a wild lurch to starboard, and rushed headlong into the abyss. I muttered a hurried prayer to God, and thought all was over.

"As I felt the sickening sweep of the descent, I had instinctively tightened my hold upon the barrel, and closed my eyes. For some seconds I dared not open them — while I expected instant destruction, and wondered that I was not already in my death-struggles with the water. But moment after moment elapsed. I still lived. The sense of falling had ceased; and the motion of the vessel seemed much as it had been before, while in the belt of foam, with the exception that she now lay more along. I took courage, and looked once again upon the scene.

"Never shall I forget the sensations of awe, horror, and admiration with which I gazed about me. The boat appeared to be hanging, as if by magic, midway down, upon the interior surface of a funnel prodigious in circumference, immeasurable in depth, and whose perfectly smooth sides might have been mistaken for ebony, but for the bewildering rapidity with which they spun around, and for the gleaming and ghastly radiance they shot forth, as the rays of the full moon, from that circular rift amid the clouds which I have already described, streamed in a flood of golden glory along the black walls, and far away down into the inmost recesses of the abyss.

"At first I was too much confused to observe anything accurately. The general burst of terrific grandeur was all that I beheld. When I recovered myself a little, however, my gaze fell instinctively downward. In this direction I was able to obtain an unobstructed view, from the manner in which the smack hung on the inclined surface of the pool. She was quite upon an even keel — that is to say, her deck lay in a plane parallel with that of the water — but this latter sloped at an angle of more than forty-five degrees, so that we seemed to be lying upon our beam-ends. I could not help observing, nevertheless, that I had scarcely more difficulty in maintaining my hold and footing in this situation, than if we had been upon a dead level; and this, I suppose, was owing to the speed at which we revolved.

"The rays of the moon seemed to search the very bottom of the profound gulf; but still I could make out nothing distinctly, on account of a thick mist in which everything there was enveloped, and over which there hung a magnificent rainbow, like that narrow and tottering bridge which Mussulmen say is the only pathway between Time and Eternity. This mist, or spray, was no doubt occasioned by the clashing of the great walls of the funnel, as they all met together at the bottom — but the yell that went up to the Heavens from out of that mist, I will not attempt to describe.

"Our first slide into the abyss itself, from the belt of foam above, had carried us a great distance down the slope; but our farther descent was by no means proportionate. Round and round we swept — not with any uniform movement — but in dizzying swings and jerks, that sent us sometimes only a few hundred yards — sometimes nearly the complete circuit of the whirl. Our progress downward, at each revolution, was very perceptible, but slow.

"Looking about me upon the wide waste of liquid ebony on which we were thus borne, I perceived that our boat was not the only object in the embrace of the whirl. Both above and below us were visible fragments of vessels, large masses of building timber and trunks of trees, with many smaller articles, such as pieces of house furniture, broken boxes, barrels and staves. I have already described the unnatural curiosity which had taken the place of my original terrors. It appeared to grow upon me as I drew nearer and nearer to my dreadful doom. I now began to watch, with a strange interest, the numerous things that floated in our company. I must have been delirious — for I even sought amusement in speculating upon the relative velocities of their several descents toward the foam below. "This fir tree," I found myself at one time saying, "will certainly be the next thing that takes the awful plunge and disappears," — and then I was disappointed to find that the wreck of a Dutch merchant ship overtook it and went down before. At length, after making several guesses of this nature, and being deceived in all — this fact — the fact of my invariable miscalculation — set me upon a train of reflection that made my limbs again tremble, and my heart beat heavily once more.

"It was not a new terror that thus affected me — but the dawn of a more exciting hope. This hope arose partly from memory, and partly from present observation. I called to mind the great variety of buoyant matter that strewed the coast of Lofoden, having been absorbed and then thrown forth by the Moskoe-ström. By far the greater number of the articles were shattered in the most extraordinary way — so chafed and roughened as to have the appearance of being stuck full of splinters — but then I distinctly recollected that there were some of them which were not disfigured at all. Now I could not account for this difference except by supposing that the roughened fragments were the only ones which had been completely absorbed — that the others had entered the whirl at so late a period of the tide, or, for some reason, had descended so slowly after entering, that they did not reach the bottom before the turn of the flood came, or of the ebb, as the case might be. I conceived it possible, in either instance, that they might thus be whirled up again to the level of the ocean, without undergoing the fate of those which had been drawn in more early, or absorbed more rapidly. I made, also, three important observations. The first was, that, as a general rule, the larger the bodies were, the more rapid their descent — the second, that, between two masses of equal extent, the one spherical, and the other of any other shape, the superiority in speed of descent was with the sphere — the third, that, between two masses of equal size, the one cylindrical, and the other of any other shape, the cylinder was absorbed the more slowly. Since my escape, I have had several conversations on this subject with an old school-master of the district; and it was from him that I learned the use of the words 'cylinder' and 'sphere.' He explained to me — although I have forgotten the explanation — how what I observed was, in fact, the natural consequence of the forms of the floating fragments — and showed me how it happened that a cylinder, swimming in a vortex, offered more resistance to its suction, and was drawn in with greater difficulty than an equally bulky body, of any form whatever.

"There was one startling circumstance which went a great way in enforcing these observations, and rendering me anxious to turn them to account, and this was that, at every revolution, we passed something like a barrel, or else the yard or the mast of a vessel, while many of these things, which had been on our level when I first opened my eyes upon the wonders of the whirlpool, were now high up above us, and seemed to have moved but little from their original station. I no longer hesitated what to do. I resolved to lash myself securely to the water-cask upon which I now held, to cut it loose from the counter, and to throw myself with it into the water. I attracted my brother's attention by signs, pointed to the floating barrels that came near us, and did everything in my power to make him understand what I was about to do. I thought at length that he comprehended my design — but, whether this was the case or not, he shook his head despairingly, and refused to move from his station by the ring-bolt. It was impossible to reach him; the emergency admitted of no delay; and so, with a bitter struggle, I resigned him to his fate, fastened myself to the cask by means of the lashings which secured it to the counter, and precipitated myself with it into the sea, without another moment's hesitation.

"The result was precisely what I had hoped it might be. As it is myself who now tell you this tale — as you see that I did escape — and as you are already in possession of the mode in which this escape was effected, and must therefore anticipate all that I have farther to say — I will bring my story quickly to conclusion. It might have been an hour, or thereabout, after my quitting the smack, when, having descended to a vast distance beneath me, it made three or four wild gyrations in rapid succession, and bearing, my loved brother with it, plunged headlong, at once and forever, into the chaos of foam below. The barrel to which I was attached sunk very little farther than half the distance between the bottom of the gulf and the spot at which I leaped overboard, before a great change took place in the character of the whirlpool. The froth and the rainbow disappeared. The slope of the sides of the vast funnel became momently less and less steep. The gyrations of the whirl grew feeble and fluctating — then ceased altogether — then finally reversed themselves with a gradually accelerating motion. And then the bottom of the gulf uprose — and its turgid aspect had in great measure departed. The sky was clear, the winds had gone down, and the full moon was setting radiantly in the west, when I found myself on the surface of the ocean, in full view of the shores of Lofoden, and above the spot where the pool of the Moskoe-ström had been. It was the hour of the slack — but the sea still heaved in mountainous waves from the effects of the hurricane. I was borne violently into the channel of the Ström, and in a few minutes was hurried down the coast into the "grounds" of the fishermen. A boat picked me up — exhausted from fatigue — and (now that the danger was removed) speechless from the memory of its horror. Those who drew me on board were my old mates and daily companions — but they knew me no more than they would have known a traveller from the spirit-land. My hair which had been raven-black the day before,and now it is white as you see. They say too that the whole expression of my countenance had changed. I told them my story — they did not believe it. I now tell it to you — and you will put no more faith in it than did the merry fishermen of Lofoden.

www.ingramcontent.com/pod-product-compliance
Lightning Source LLC
Chambersburg PA
CBHW032152020726
47496CB00003B/834